ROPE

DANCES

ROPE DANCES

Fictions by

David Porush

FICTION COLLECTIVE, INC.   NEW YORK

The author wishes to thank the Literature and Writing Sections of the Department of Humanities of M.I.T. for a summer writing grant which in part made these stories possible.

All characters in this book are fictional.

This publication is in part made possible with support from the National Endowment for the Arts in Washington, D.C., a Federal agency, the New York State Council on the Arts, Brooklyn College, and the Teachers and Writers Collaborative.

Published by FICTION COLLECTIVE, INC.
Production by Coda Press, Inc.
Distributed by: George Braziller, Inc.
One Park Avenue
New York, N.Y. 10016

For my family.

"Add to these allurements, mute and still,
Others of a wider scope, where living men,
Music, and shifting pantomimic scenes,
Together joined their multifarious aid
To heighten the allurement. . .
I more than once
Here took my seat, and maugre frequent fits
Of irksomeness, with ample recompense
Saw singers, rope-dancers, giants and dwarfs,
Clowns, conjurors, posture-masters, harlequins,
Amid the uproar of the babblement,
Perform their feats."

William Wordsworth, *The Prelude* (1805).

CONTENTS

I
FRAYED THREADS

II
DREAM STRINGS

III
ROPE DANCES

    1. The Game: A Description
    2. They Play
    3. Tug-of-War

I

FRAYED THREADS

KING KONG DISMEMBERED

King Kong Recipe
Time: 32 min.   *Serves: 1*

1 pair of scissors
1 roll scotch tape
1 short story, "King Kong Dismembered"
1 large room
1 working electric fan

With pair of scissors, cut out each page of the short story, "King Kong Dismembered," along the edge of the page closest to the binding. Caution: do not slice any words. Turn on the electric fan in one corner of the large room. Holding the sheets loosely in the left hand, sprinkle the pages lightly in front of the fan and watch as they are blown across the room. Collect the sheets in the order of their distance from the walls, the closest first. In this new order, scotch tape the sheets back into the book and begin reading King Kong. No two recipes exactly alike.

A giant ape, man. An ape. God! An Almighty ape.

Through
High branch dark scattering
See Silver Woman
In woman time
shine fulsome, ripe fruit
            open and soft

to take / KONG WANTS / to take

Premonition becomes admonition
And godhead is no good
Unless Kong can control Kong's dreams
            moonlight
            moans and high whinnies
            ferocious paleness of new consort

WHAT DOES
KONG WANT

Stir little monster
And wriggle, you
Antediluvian fish
Between the thighs of a most powerful ONE
Tell me what you have divined
From the scented drippings
From little birds' behinds
On a jungle leaf.

ONE / Cannot explain loneliness to / ONE

Nor are the poetries of an ape
No matter how large
Feasible
For even the smallest moment
Not a bit.

Friday, August 13

The island is only a few days away. The crew is holding up pretty well, though they're looking unruly and scurvous. Tight as a harem. In fact, their nocturnal habits are none of my business, officially, but it's not an uncommon sight to see these men holding hands behind the chimneys, or snatching a quick buss before mess, pinching each other's tight sailor bottoms. One has to wonder, though, how they manage at night in the narrow berths; the doubling up can be damn noisy, too. Look, they've got me fantasizing, excited, damn them. Well, they need their fun, need to let off some steam. It's been a weird voyage, bound to get weirder. Still, you got to wonder when you see a three hundred pound mate blushing like a schoolgirl because some other lubber touched his hand in passing a bowl of mush at mess.

—*From the private diary of Capt. Englehorn (1929)*

King Kong is a fat and ungainly beast. In his head though, he watches himself, his image of himself, act out a graceful life in the role of a sleek cat, a lithesome, sloe-eyed stud. When he awakes in the morning he rolls over on his bed and stretches his body, his overlong arms guiding an almost-human hand in caresses of solipsism over his matted fur. His yawns create small storms. Pterodactyls circle lazily overhead; his natural enemies, they have been plaguing his lair for generations. He makes a mental note to kill some every day, but forgets as soon as they drift out of sight, stupidly, since he cannot make even imaginary notes on imaginary pads without an opposable thumb.

Kong's genius lies elsewhere, though. He has an inordinate eye for symmetry, beauty. Item: One human-hair rug, knotted four hundred times to the square inch, which impressed with the weight of his body twice a day for centuries, can be read as a text of suffering and eroticism.

Kong is a profound sentimentalist. Human skulls, mementos riven from the heads of former lovers, adorn his room. In them he toasts his exhausted victims before he kills them; they writhe, then fall silent, under his dark eyes. If he remembers these moments it is with a memory unlike ours. An incipient stirring in the loins? A tingling wisp of sensation in the head? A spark of synaptic accident in the brain? No matter. Preening himself with the utmost care way into midday, Kong finally clambers down the sheer cliff to look for food.

Sometime this morning the anchors were dropped. A calm familiar throbbing in an endless sea has been replaced by something more insidious, a little more dangerous; a subtle wind blows from off an unseen coast. The fog thickens everything, including thought. I know; I was on watch last night. I smelled that tinge of fecund taint that meant we were approaching land. Now, in the hold, with the pitch of the boat a little less predictable, the shore cannot be far off. Why am I afraid to go above and check the scene for myself?

"When Captain Englehorn came up to me in Shanghai I was lying slut-sick against a wall, propped by a bottle of gin under my arm.

"The drums have started.

"The little slope-eyed bastards had stripped me of everything worth taking. I just got out of jail. There was a living sore in my side: leeches the size of my finger, large blood-sucking fat parasites wriggled in the open wound, eating my flesh. I ran a fever, a delirious death-dive much more profound than the chronic malarial flush that all us white men endure in this hellhole climate. I drank gin, gin so potent it killed most of the mothers in my side as I bathed them with the crazy juice. They slid drunkenly down my side and were already drying up in the sun, turning black as death on the smooth stones of the yellow man's pavement.

"The Captain knew me, of course. We had steamed out together in '17, my first ride on the *Justine* before she was rammed and bottomed by the Japanese invading China. Again in '22 on the *Naked Lunch* which went twice around the Pacific and once around the Cape before the Brooklyn yards stole it from us. Yeah, those were the days of boat rustlers, that's right, those foreigner sailor-cowboys, wild seamen who would swoop down on whole fleets of stray schooners, steamers, unguarded oilers, fishers, gibbering in Italian or Espanol or Norway, down and out sailor toughs signed on by the big boat yards, even the Navy, to get scrap metal, spare parts, anything that would stay afloat, empty hulls, no questions asked. Yeah, like all the worldly goods of this Jeremy after the slopes got to them that gin afternoon, the Naked Lunch is spread over this goddamned watery world.

"The drums have begun. Once they start they shan't yield 'til a man's head is filled with the noise that drives . . . once they start. . . .

"So, when the Captain comes up to me he was not surprised at this old soak Jeremy, not too, I don't think. He puffed on his pipe, slung me round his shoulder and dragged me to the *Faye Wray* where I was nursed, for days, by a pair of legs bustling round my bed.

"Eerie sea-fog and the drums, sleep and drums, drums and sleep, both hard to endure."

> —*Interview with Jeremy Wimpers, first mate of the Faye Wray, by Jules Englehorn, Asian scholar and Ph.D candidate at U. of Hawaii.*

Kong smells his prey before he hears her screams.

Sensitive creature. The high wilting quality, the fragility in the desperate wails are new to him. Her protests follow a beat that lures him down from his cliffside lair.

Wary lizards, fourteen feet long, swing slowly away, hissing their brute resentment. Lidless eyes gaze at the jungle, turning inwards, then, refusing to acknowledge, but afraid not to, the passing of royalty. Grace of a fluid mountain, familiar path.

Sensitive ageless beast hears the beckoning of screams, reads the lure behind the siren, the new calm note that the sacrifice strains for in her frenzy.

As sure as the single eternal gesture of the whore beckoning to her john, the beauty speaks to the beast now --Come-------------------------- sings to him. Kong feels the warm breath in his ear, though he is still furlongs away. Friction of fur on fur heats his thighs --------------------------Here I am------------------------------------ In a thousand thousand years he hasn't felt this eager --------------------------------Virgin--------------------yours-------- his walk turns to a slow trot, loping race with anticipation --forever-------------------take me------------------------away-------------my soft mouth---------- (((aaah at last long moon time strange SILVER mother this one fights a little snake drink her up smell take devour good KONG WANTS)))

One man perched atop the enormous wall sighted a fist raised against the moon, blotting it out. The native screamed a ritualized wail, a wail which bore uncanny resemblances to those squeals of horror and fascination that would be uttered in a movie theater years and oceans away.

Behind the ancient wall the natives danced, sweated, danced furiously. A mother sang out, fell to the ground, frothed at the mouth, and a circle gathered around her for an instant; but no, she is not potent enough to hold their sway against the better show promised them by the contortions of a black virgin pinned to the altar outside the walls, outside the walls . . . but no, this woman is not potent enough to hold their sway, their centrifugal, communal tension and the tribe is flung out to continue spinning, colliding with each other and their fates; and though a man died in hysterical fear, and another man, an idiot, a clown with one bad leg beat himself in the face, punched his own head as his mother looked on with execrations and urges, it is clear that some other force must hold them, create their world anew; they await some larger god omened by the Fist against the Moon and a virginal consort who fainted against the cold stone.

Native bodies contorted in shapes strange to human geometry. Their dance was their ticket to the upcoming show.

Folks on 52nd St. and 5th Ave. lined up around the block. Matrons already inside the theatre held lorgnettes and fiddled with heavy pearl necklaces that heaved on enormous bosoms. Men passed sceptical remarks, lit their cigars.

"The papers say it's this guy, what's his name, you know, the jungle movie man, uh, Denham, yeah. It's Denham pulling off another one of his scams."

"They say chimpanzees are very smart."

"Yeah, but did you see those teeth? Those fangs must have been six feet high."

"But his eye looked so human, like a child's."

"That's what the jojo's say. Bad medicine. Bad, bad medicine."

"That landlubbin' shitlickin' Denham. That cocksucker."

"Look, sonny. Without Denham, ther'd be no Annie. And I seen the way ye been lookin' a' that piece. Now, it's none o' my mess, but if it were my fish that were wrigglin' on that hook . . ."

"Ah, shut up, ya old scurve. It ain't yer fish, cause yer fish ain't waggled at nothin' fer years. So just shut up, ya old scurve."

"Still, bad medicine is bad medicine. And the jojos know this sea, and they say there's somethin' on that island, and . . ."

"And, and, and, and . . ."

"Motherfuckin' Denham."

People up front cower as Kong's ugly mug loomed in front of them. Kong blinks in the dark of the theater.

Men and boys who have stayed a third time to see the movie are still amazed when the natives close the giant gates and leave the virgin Anne at the fingertips of the jungle. The woman is a blurred luminescent speck: she writhes in a fearful delirium against a dark surround. The rags on her body, tatters of her dress torn in the struggle against her shackles, part. The full moon strikes her bare belly. The belly, exposed to the sky, is as round as the moon. One thigh lifts in an eternal pose of acceptance, her legs slightly parted. Her mouth falls open, the lips pout, her tongue dashes across them. And, only for a second, for an eye-defying temptation of an instant, her breast bobbles, quivers in the moonlight before she rolls over on her side with a moan. The boys in the theatre gazed as the single nipple—bloody-dark—rose against a sure death.

"Did you see that?" one whispered. A friend nodded, too excited to speak.

The drums have driven the men crazy. Hearing the throb and base-line beat of a people mapping the genital throb of a cosmos made the sailors on a puny ship moored outside the island reef want to tear their ears off in agony.

That night they heard the first mate's screams in the brig. Wilton cried through his drool and rammed his head again and again into the walls, moaning until a superstitious guard took pity and knocked him unconscious with an unheard apology: "Sorry old friend."

And Miss Farrell. Miss Farrell the starlet, the whore, the foredeck strumpet paraded on the deck, swinging her hips to some rhythm, tuning in to some unutterable jive. The lickings of her lips and the spread of her thighs, the drip of moisture between her breasts were the lyrics to a monstrous song that drove these men-wrecks upon private shoals. What siren duet did she play with the island? Why did she seem to be the mysterious force for whom the drums played?

Kong's needs merge and blur into each other. He cannot distinguish among them. When his belly is empty his enormous cock rises like a cyclopean serpent, as though it could divine food through its more sensitive and consuming need. When he is hurt he moans in a song, a bass string across which a bow is drawn for long moments. His note vibrates in the bowels of birds. Trees shake. The semi-active volcano at the center of the island smokes in sympathy.

The natives say, "It Kongs."

They've given over eight-tenths of their habitat to this beast deity. They are unable to decide whether Kong is sacred or profane, so they strike a fair middle though AMBIGUOUS course and send him their virgins to deflower. Only withered and half-dead old women and the mad may fling dead dogs over the wall in contempt, no, not so much for the tyrant himself, but for his cousin, Death.

In January, 1976 Jules Englehorn, grandson of Captain Robert Englehorn—a commander and owner of the infamous ship that brought a giant ape to New York City in 1932—found this entry in the old man's diary:

> *Don't think I don't have my reservations about this project. Yes, I have my ambitions, too. But I'm an educated man. The lure of cash shouldn't have overwhelmed me like that. I'm an old romantic fool looking for a last adventure to tell the grandchildren.*

Jules, fascinated and depressed, looked up from the manuscript to wipe away a tear.

> *Well, there's no turning back, no. Carl Denham gave me the old soft sell, touched my soft spot. Hidden treasures. Native tales. Monsters. No, I was stupid, but Denham's dangerous, with his passion for despoiling these sad men, my crew, corrupting them for his militant art. He's looking for this monster he says, to graft its fantastic limbs and head onto an art, a vision, a movie. But who in hell needs a madman's blather to be sprayed in two dimensions? Why will his film-myth stir the loins more than little Annie Farrell? Will his movie darken the mind more than demon drums? Yet he will give over Anne to sluttish beauty and sacrifice her to the celluloid monster, the Silver Screen Beast.*

It inspired him to begin his dissertaion on the oral tradition among sailors, an investigation of their folklore and the history of their mythology. He was a Ph.D. candidate at the University of Hawaii.

The drums stopped at the height of their madness.

Hundreds of warriors lined the walls.

Anne's moans could barely be heard. She had exhausted herself screaming. Natives looked to the jungle in anticipation. We white men were forgotten in the hush which fell over the scene.

Then I heard a sound which haunts me now, and I shudder just to think of it. A combination of all the hellish groans, screams, whispers, suffering cries, lamentations, and desperate moans mankind has uttered in his many generations. In the bellowing triumph of the monster could be heard all the doggish animal whines, brutish thick-tongued ejaculations of suffering of a species dying even as it emerges from its cave. I stood transfixed by the reflection of my own evolution recorded in a momentary utterance.

We rushed to the chinks in the wall while the natives, possessed by superstitious fear, lay prostrate, trembling.

A giant ape, larger than our ship, stood in a small clearing around the stone slab on which poor Anne lay.

He stood straddling the altar, his enormous anatomy dangling over her body, beating his chest again and again, singing.

He bent down to his victim, his face as large as the sky. All my desire tingled in the horror of the moment, spurred by the illumination of a full moon shining on the phantasmagoric scene.

I must have been mad.

I thought I saw Anne smile up at him and wink. Her mind has snapped, that must have been it, I told myself, her mind has snapped.

Kong snapped her bonds, held her aloft, high over his head, she emerged from the middle of his clenched fist: in the conjunction of their poses I saw the mocking salute of beauty and the beast telling the world to go fuck itself.

Certainly, there are portions of the movie "King Kong" that are more interesting than the ones recounted in this fictional fragmentation.

King Kong presented to a group of photographers.

King Kong unchained.

King Kong scaling the man-made cliff, the Empire State Building, grasping the innocent Anne Farrell (a.k.a. Faye Wray). Anne, a mere toy in his paw, pathetic, erotic, wriggles, screams, faints.

King Kong derailing the trains, knocking them off the el, establishing a precedent for all other monsters who ritually, gratuitously, also knock trains off their tracks (Godzilla, Rodan, et al.).

King Kong swatting at mechanical pterodactyls who spit fire and hurt, who are more relentless, more streamlined and efficient, guided by a newer intelligence. No longer the idiot creatures of his fatherland, these birds buzz and hurt.

I like that. I like the fact that Kong escapes to terrorize the very people who have created him; Kong escapes from the theatre to waste the city streets; Kong escapes from the screen to haunt the nights of Hollywood producers, scripters, actors, terrorizing their urbanity with his monstrous obscenity, his natural unnaturalness.

"Beauty and the Beast!" shouted Carl Denham.

The photographers exploded bulbs in his face.

Miss Farrell confidently approached her enormous paramour.

New Yorkers emerge from the theater, blinking their eyes in front of the marquee, sweeping the skyline with sensitive vision, hoping they would see the Kong towering above them. Years later they are still unable to pass the Empire State Building without pointing out the spire, remembering the movie, perhaps searching the wall for bullet holes from the spray of the fighter planes' guns.

And just as there were parts of the movie that were, perhaps, more stirring, so are there parts of Captain Englehorn's diary which are more relevant, and parts of the madness on this ship which are more relevant, and more surreal, and more brutal. And, certainly, the native ritual to Kong is not as important as the pathos of the virgin and her thoughts, nor do they describe the mundane flavor of native existence on Skull Island.

Finally, Kong, too, has lugged himself through more interesting days, performed more emblematic actions, conjured in his own plodding way more exotic thoughts and taunts and intercourses, earlier morning risings, greater success against the pterodactyls.

((so what if you thought that this passage or that coda was good bad indifferent boring gratuitous or if you tired of the adjectives and endless verbal indulgences indemnifications identifications reiterations vociferations exhortations reifications))

This grand game poses questions, and just as my characters have had better days, more enticing alternatives . . . those infinite choices are mine, too, and the whole project poses certain questions, like:

Why are there no characters, no plot, no theme except one of desire, that desire the character, the plot, the theme, the sole actor, the narrator, the motif? And how or why should any desire to know about Kong—or about the native dancers who dance for him or about the virgin imbued with heroic knowledge as she is about to be sacrificed or about Anne who is jealous of the virgin or about the crew members jealous of each other or about Captain Englehorn who watches the crew

and Annie and the island and perceives a drama unfolding about the audience which cowers in front of the Big Lie or about Jules Englehorn, Asian scholar embarked on a quest to reconstruct the history of his grandfather's voyage or about the narrator who selects and chooses and stylizes and hems and haws and pretends and dances and hits himself in the face with his typewriter and uses language as enormous as his subject and watches his own writing slump and pull down its pants and micturate on his ambitions?
Huh? Why?

II

DREAM STRINGS

THE SOMNAMBULISTS

"Keep looking at me or maybe my words will go all to pieces."
—Rudyard Kipling, "The Man Who Would be King"

Do dreams have meaning? No, not when you are a twin, are twinned by some monster who is dreaming for you, when you wake in the middle of the dream and find that you are someone else's nightwalker. And dreams don't dream. No. How many times can you dream the same character, the one who seems so much like you and is doomed to walk through your night with a sigh and an empty gaze, because he has no night, no sleep, no searing messages burnt across the cerebral synapses, no night, no dream? But the imagination of him is a gothic one, is fretted and frescoed and arabesqued by the punctures made in us by light and day.

25

Beauty is a vehicle for nightmare, a point of disarming cyclop's vision that drives through unnamed barriers and then looks out when you're not looking out through your own horrified eye.

Beauty is a celestial stag trapped in its purity until released by miners, malicious seekers after truth. With a silent look the stag dissolves into foam that spreads pestilential waves over the surface of the earth.

Beauty is a simple salmon, fights against the stream of consciousness to deposit its eggs in a spawning pool. Salmon eggs hatch. Monstrous Progeny! They swim away, all teeth, eating the river as they go, abolishing time; piranhas, these spawned cannibals/they eat mother/then each other/Sharks!/ they are ancient/eat up love/lie in wait/scenting my bloody dreams they move in.

Trying to tell myself to WAKE UP! I sleep more deeply, WAKE UP! I swim, plunge, thrash about, drowndream, WAKE UP! cry in my sleep inconsolably. Don't die, wake up, sit up in bed, stare ahead, find I am still sleeping, my eyes scare my girlfriend who is bitchy at seven o'clock in the morning. She walked the streets all night, got her bottom pinched (You would be a bitch, too, if you had a sore ass), but she wakes up too, though she wishes she were asleep and sees, now, that something is really wrong. I cried, and she caressed my chest, my hair. My hair all wet, I wanted to tear my clothing. When a man begins mourning he should tear his clothing to show that the fabric of his life is torn.

I WANTED TO SIT SEVEN DAYS on a hard bench and pour ashes on my head and tear my clothes. But for whom? Anyway, I was naked; hot and naked and didn't want to tear my skin.

She knew I liked to drive, so despite the fact she'd had only an hour's sleep we bundled up and got into her car. Dead of the winter it was, but I had the wild idea to put the hood down in her convertible, to convert my life against the incontrovertible proof of grief.

"You're still disturbed."

"Of course I'm still disturbed, you bitch."

"O.K., O.K. Look, I'm sorry. Let's drive around."

"That's what we're doing."

"I said I'm sorry."

"O.K.," she said. Pause. "You didn't have to get so angry."

"I'm not angry!" I screamed. "Will you just drive the damned car?"

"O.K. But not if you yell."

"I won't yell. I'm sorry."

"O.K. Forget it."

"O.K."

We drove another mile, crossed a river over the steel-fretted finery of an old railroad bridge.

"You frighten me."

I huddled deeper in the seat and wished I had a drink. I tried to close off my senses, rubbed by sandpaper. Then I recognized the route we had to take, the route dictated and ordained by a cipher only I understood. The car rolled along on the empty streets and my day began to look like a string of stop lights, a string of false dawn red suns. Pimps waved at me from passing cars too big to be named. Taxi drivers shot up, lay back, got off. The dispatch lady, singing over their radios, pretended to be a rock star. The junkie hacks pretended, too. Middle of the night.

"Take this turn," I said to her.

"You didn't have to call me a bitch."

"Take this turn, will you?" It was urgent. I saw a necklace of green lights reflecting off the ice of the streets beckoning me with the promise of future dreamless nights to come. It was so much like a movie seen through the dark of anxiety.

An ambulance passed by, wailing in the morning, the Rican driver blasting the siren just for the hell of it, for spite, because it's dawn and he's up while the world sleeps, because he's high, because he saw my beautiful friend in the driver's seat next to a heap of brown rags and wanted to impress her.

"Wonder where they're going?" I asked.

I needed to see, too, because of that innate superstition that follows tragedy: that is, if someone else is dying, then I'm not. I mean, that feeling that there but for the grace of God go I. In fact, that's me and not me, the other, my tragic twin, the perpetual fall guy. This feeling makes me laugh. *He's* dying, *he* got his leg shot off, *his* wife can't keep her thighs closed, *his* baby is brain damaged, *his* mother masturbates, not me HA HA, not me. Not my leg, wife, baby, mother. His heart palpitates, he needs insulin, thorazine, a fix, a poke in the eye with a pointed stick, a slap in the belly with a wet fish, an ass wipe, a tampax for his mouth, a crutch for his crotch, HA HA not me, whoooeee, there I go (ALMOST). Poor guy! (I wipe the tears from my eye yiyiyiyi, what a card, put him in the sideshow, will ya? Look, he's better than the siamese twins, and look where they're connected. In the head, yes. What a draw. What a crowd pleaser. A real geek. Just give him a drink and he'll be quiet and swallow the heads of live chickens.) So we followed the ambulance.

"Look, you're frightening me. Let's go home."

"Follow the ambulance, bitch."

"No, please, jesus. Look, I'll give you the car, then you can go ahead. Please."

I moved closer to her, excited, threw the blanket off my lap and put my arm around her. "You're doing fine. Just go faster. Don't lose him. Damn, he turned up ahead. Faster."

"What's gotten into you? I don't understand what you're doing and I want to go home." She started crying, quietly, blinking away the tears so she could see the road, crying, which gave me a certain cruel pleasure. I even loved her then, in proportion to my cruelty.

* * *

The lake opened up before us, an unfrozen expanse of fluid funhouse mirror. We had driven for hours, desperately. Night had already fallen long before. Jennifer (was that her name? Jennifer?) was past crying. I think she caught a bit of my desperation; perhaps the ragged edge of my flapping

28

compulsion fanned her too, and she drove rigidly following my directions. We arrived an hour or so later than the ambulance, but by that time I had tuned in and knew where to go and what was coming. Knew and not knew, that is. Knew like you know when as you pack that last scotch away in the evening and, half passed out, your guts are already scripting the coming program of dreams. So when the Big Fear comes upon you, it is not less fearful for its familiarity, but more fearful for its terrible accuracy.

Lights were tricking across the lake, red and blue, flashing an urgent code. From hundreds of yards away the call of police radios, sharp squawks of some fascist grammar, bounced off the lake to us. Boats lay stiffly at attention, seemed to be slowly sinking. They were well-lit and all of them full of life but for one, the last one, which had an enormous, luminescent Star on its side. As Jennifer and I got out of the car I could hear a babble of languages from the boats, a cacaphony, a confused polyglot, but from the Star boat, wails in a tongue more alien and deathly, a wailing groancurse,

". . . *bechaychon oveyomeychon ovechayay dechol base* . . ." I mouthed the words to myself.

To our left I saw a group of policemen tugging at a rope. They stood on a sheer embankment ten feet high while two cops balanced on a ladder pressed against the muddy sides, its bottom rungs under the lake water. With a terrible clarity I could see them haul on the ropes. Bubbles, lit from underneath, burst in eruptions of light as a gurgle broke across the water, strangely out of sync with the light. A green, bloated face neared the surface, and I could see a goggle-eyed corpse swimming on its back by the ladder. Uncanny! It floated by itself. Then a green frogman emerged like some flippery crustacean pushing the corpse—his twin—before him.

Jennifer hugged me and averted her eyes, whispering, "Oh, God. Did you see that?" But I was oblivious to her touch and voice, cloaked in guilt. I felt somehow responsible and began to understand the urgency of our drive through the day.

"If only we had gotten here sooner," I said. "I told you to

drive faster, hag."

"If I had driven any faster we would have been in real trouble. Didn't you see the police behind us?" Her eyes flooded again.

"I was too intent on the road. Now don't you start up again." It was true. For the first time I felt the ache behind my eyes as my head began to reel. The lake, the flashing lights, grotesque corpses and boats were strangely beautiful: they were arranged in a pattern of symbols that was familiar, that encoded something deep, but too deep to reach, quite. I closed my eyes, trying to remember, trying to decipher the code. Boats, lake, lights, the faces of the dead . . . A code from which something was missing. When I opened my eyes, I still could not bear to look at the intense scene, so for the first time I scanned the shore. I saw then that all the people milling around, the curious, the horror hoarders, were freaks, the kind of freaks that populate one's worst nights. They weren't physical monsters, no, not midgets, bearded ladies, siamese twins, quadriplegiacs, mongoloids, strippers who smoked cigarettes with their cunts, he-shes, geeks, golems, no. They were freaks of human nature. These people paraded through the corrupt night (it had gotten so dark that by now the flashing lights were necessary, the ghostly ship lights gleamed across the water, piercing through the dark sensations of death) lounging in their bathing suits and sunglasses. Some relaxed on chaises or blankets, reading newspapers, though it was hardly light enough to see your own feet. Not even a moon out to explain this lunacy. They all seemed impervious to the horror on the lake, chatted in small groups, listened to the AM radio. Bathing suits! I was freezing. In my excitement I had left the car without my blanket, and my skin was covered with gooseflesh, my teeth began to rattle. I leaned closer to Jennifer for warmth, leaned further over, my body seeking hers, leaned over to her and fell down. In a panic I wheeled around but saw her closer to the shore watching corpses rise to the surface.

"Look. They all have the same face."

"What do you mean they all have the same face? You're as blind as an asshole." I wanted it desperately not to be true. But I looked, and indeed, all the faces were alike, the face of my twin. It struck me then that this was my brother's lake. All the mysteries of my own actions now became explicable. This was why I was so furiously compelled to come here, why everything seemed so familiar yet new, somehow. But the mystery of the connection eluded me. I felt like someone dreaming, seeing themselves in the middle of a great coniferous forest and shouting, arms spread wide, gleefully, "I am in Chicago!" The illogic is never questioned by the dreamed, but the dreamer remarks to himself, "That's O.K. I am in bed and this is the logic of dreams." Was I now at the lake, or was I dreaming? Was I not home in bed, my thighs barely gracing the flesh behind Jennifer's knees as she slept? I recalled my twinship. Doubleheaded halved by life, squared by thought, rooted in the singularity of doubleness. The duplicity of our face had always been cause for comment. Passing each other in a darkened hallway created a mirror. I could not stand to see his eyes, would lose myself. His touch was the most exciting in the world: pressing his cheek with mine had the intimacy of sex without the heat. Together we were monstrous, and monsters should be killed by the tribe because they portend evil. (Our tribe kills us with anxiety.) We had never experienced loneliness. Sympathy also was alien to us. The world assumed our twinship was a supreme consolation. My thoughts swam in the wake of another's whose thoughts swam in the wake of mine. We had always swirled each other's lives around, striving in each other's orbits. And now, once again. He had returned. I had returned.

CAN YOU IMAGINE WHAT IT IS LIKE TO FEAR SOMEONE ELSE'S DEATH AS MUCH AS YOUR OWN? Not more or less but exactly as much? To turn black and blue because your other self has bumped his leg? To have no refuge in altruism or solipsism?

The word 'our' had lost its meaning. The word 'I' became an abstraction, a partial differential equation.

My life suffered for the sharing of it. My resentment was a fugitive that eluded me as I tried to articulate it, because my style was cramped by ambiguity, ambi-valence: my pulse given impulse; my shadow given body; my reflex given action; my reflection given act; my auto, mobility; my *sui, generis*; my ego, other; my I, sight; part—partner, vision—revision, cognition—recognition, and my only lament reduced to a two-part harmony:

My other brother has his druthers,
His druthers are also mine.
Both wish there had been none other,
So one could draw the line.

Two heads, it's said, are good as one,
But one is best of all,
For my every run is re-run,
My every call recalled.

My every flux is his reflex;
His every course my curse.
This very text that you hear next
Has a former verse reversed.

One head they say is better than two,
And one far better than none,
But what we do as a duo
Alone becomes undone.

Oh doppelganger! Oh other brother! Oh ghost! Oh geist!
Oh guest!
Oh double-headed! Oh self-other! Twinned life is a
grand jest!
My other brother has a twin brother
His brother is also mine
Both wish that we had had another
Go back to the first line.

A body still floated by the base of the ladder. Faces still rose to the surface amid bubbles of light. Now the yachts lined up on the lake were playing music, all except the one with the Star on its side. A latin beat, the sound of marimbas and flutes and the high, quick chatter of Puerto Ricans became confused with the pornophony of Motown, a polka, a Verdi opera, all the music blending into one mad din, like an ethnic war of tunes punctuated by squeals of drunken ladies and the splash of another body falling into the lake. Perhaps they were rehearsing the sacrificial rites they had performed earlier. From the Star yacht the fervent murmurings increased until the outrage became a profound wail. The bizarre night bathers still lounged around the shore. One woman held a foil reflector under her chin, her skin gleaming darkly with the slick suntan lotion.

There was something erotic about this madness. Jennifer seemed totally vulnerable, baffled. I wanted to grab her, hold her down and loose my tongue over the psychescape of her breasts, mount her nipple, eat her hair with my fingers, lick her clit, try to climb back between her slim maternal thighs and nestle there for a long while.

I fell asleep on the cot after trying to make love to Jennifer. We had crawled into one of the bungalows too tired to bother with the mechanics of the thing, so we merely fell asleep in each other's arms. But I slept fitfully and was put half-awake, or what I thought was half-awake, by the voice of my nemesis whispering in my ear. The face hovered above my bed, as though he were bending from the waist to lean over me. I tried to touch him but felt my arms bound to my sides. No, I didn't really want to touch him, to assert his presence, to make him palpable, although his voice had a threat in it, a tension in the whisper that reminded me that it was I who abandoned *him*. His face was still smooth, though the shadows gave it an unaccustomed fierceness.

"I dreamt all this, on the lake, before it happened," he murmured. "The first night I was here I fell into a sleep as deep as yours is now and found myself wandering around a deserted trailer park; the trailers were all gutted, burnt out, rolled over on their sides. From the woods behind, gunshots. I awoke the next morning and found that two trailers had parked in a little clearing across the lake.

"A week later I had a dream about a swarm of termites devouring the forest on the west side of the lake where Moon's Mountain slopes down into it. The next day, a Monday, a crew of lumbermen started clearing land on the Moon side, human termites."

"Oh, brother."

From outside I could hear poker chips clattering against each other.

"Pair of threes, flushing . . . straight without the eight . . . nothing here, how come you're still in . . . looks high . . . pair of ladies . . ."

"A quarter."

"See it."

"Raise two bits."

The lure of the litany was overwhelming. I got off the cot and went over to the window. On the patio in front of the bungalow, perfect-bodied boys sat at a round umbrella table. The open umbrella seemed to illuminate the scene like an exposed lightbulb would, making the circle of players appear two-dimensional against the dark surround. When I stared hard at them I saw the heads on their bodies were outsized; two smoked fat cigars as though mocking their fathers.

"I'm out, ladies." A homosexual lilt made them titter.

"I'll see that and bump it a quarter."

"See it."

But they *were* their fathers: the big heads were adult heads. The faces were lined and slouched with the cynical resignation of fifty-year-olds. One face had enormous jowls which shook every time it spoke.

"Me too."

"My ace is good and I got two more underneath, boys. Get out while the getting's good. Bump ya half dollar."

Another had the bulbous, misshapen nose of a terminal alcoholic. Indeed, he drank greedily from a bottle at his side. I was scared, swore the light was playing tricks on my eyes and crawled back into bed with Jennifer.

"You should see what's going on out there."

"I saw, I saw. Go back to sleep."

I went back to sleep. The voice started talking to me again. "Every time I went to sleep it got freakier and more grotesque. Another family of Chinese, another troupe of night bathers. My dreams became more and more complicated. I woke screaming and sweating. I tried not to sleep. I drank pots of coffee, shot crystal meth, but no matter what I would try, around one o'clock in the morning an overwhelming weariness came upon me. By the time I started groping for my bed through the desirous haze, I'd already be riding my nightmares. *Dead babies floating in the water . . . an army of horse-sized rats . . . lights flashing all night . . . men in raincoats . . . and the faces!* Those poker players over there? They are the result of an afternoon's nap.

"This evening they all ganged up on that one boat. All the others dressed as pirates, stuck shivs and switchblades in their teeth, garottes in their shirts, and boarded the boats. Ffffft." He drew his finger across his throat.

* * *

Moist melting from the groin of love lulls the wanting twin jennifer sweetens the load of sleep by pullullating my penis as she breathes the warm timpanis of her honey jar caress and throb me
SIREN SCREECHING SCREAM BLOOD BOILING IN BRAIN

I awoke, jerking myself loose from Jennifer's crotch. I heard shouts and the nauseating thud of flesh on flesh and the nightmare crack of breaking bone. A scream made me cry.

35

I pulled my pants on and rushed out to the patio. The poker players were gone, but in their place: a mass of limbs and hating, sneering faces . . . the sickness in a gloaming eye . . . knives reaching into the air and descending . . . a fist poised at the height of its arc . . . a symphony of a body breaking . . . two dribbles of blood . . . love pirates . . . eye-patches and bandannas, moustaches painted on or waxed . . . a yell muffled by flesh died to a whimper . . . hands around a neck, many hands, the head . . . the face . . . the face was . . .

"Kill me!" I screamed. "Me! Me! Me! You've got the wrong one! Me!"

My twin's neck stretched, his head extended over the back of the lounge chair as the pirates punched and kicked his face blood red, then white, his face turned towards me, his eye looking into mine voicing an unspeakable resentment, an ageless communion across space of minds twinned by night, creating a last assurance of ultimacy, of unfettered calm, of accusations branding me with the guilt of the survivor as his eyes bulged in a last paroxysm, eyes rolled up into his head, the whites also bleeding, a gurgle in the throat, the "pup" of an exploded lung, a last look, a purse of the lips like a good brotherly kiss, a farewell.

Photographers snapped pictures as my twin was killed. Music blared from the boats. Lightbulbs exploded in a strobe. The nightbathers threw off their swimsuits to plunge into the lake for a collective skinny dip, and the pirates began tossing my corpse in the air. Some Indians saw the chaotic civilization which had erupted on their shores, shuddered with a tribal shrug of resignation, let their feathers fall gently to earth, and turned away. Ex-gods walked among the somnambulists, hoping to become anonymous, as they already were, with a sigh and an empty gaze (wake up) because they had no night and no dreams (Wake up!) were all dreams (WAKE UP!) floated to the surface like bloated corpses WAKE UP walked through my night WAKE UP still do, as I sleep, wake up.

VENETIAN BLIND

Of all of us who grew up outside Venice, I understood U best. I was his most faithful friend, and I was the one who, when he finally began to go strange, (as I always knew he would, though I wouldn't call his strangeness strange; it was Venice that was strange. No, rather it was all of the whole cornfield state that was strange, the whole country, yes, was strange. It was a strange time unlike any other had ever been, I knew, and in this strangest of times, I say) I was the one who understood U's jealousy best.

All of us, U and Washer and the others, and me, the Fat Man, all of us agreed that women were . . . well, let us leave the question of women aside for the moment. We had made a pact that women were . . . it's no good, there's no way one can avoid the subject . . . women were, well, *untrustworthy!* This unspoken assent was part of our mismanaged misogyny that drove us to distraction and drunkenness when one of our group finally succumbed to marriage. ("I couldn't help it," the victim would say. "I got her pregnant." "Yeah, yeah," we would sneer, and turn away from him as he pleaded with us. "The bitch lied to me, I tell you." And then the ritual replies:

"Famous last words," Washer would say. "It won't be the last time," U, always the bitterest among us, would laugh, with a cruel edge in his throat.) Yes, they all succumbed finally, until there was no one left except for U and me, the Fat Man.

I'll account for myself first. I admit I was afraid. My wrists were weak. Still are. My pants—always too ornate and too loose for this gray and tight town. I am always sucking or chewing or drinking or nibbling or biting into something. If I don't eat every twenty-five minutes, I get the bends, I begin to feel like I'm drowning. It's the same feeling I get when I'm with a woman for the first (and last) time, and I'm alone in her bed: when she slides over my enormous belly and tries to find the functional piece and as she straddles my rolling, shapeless thighs with her legs and as she eases down onto my machine— then I wonder why I am not home in my own bed by myself and I'm sure that someone is trying to reach me on the phone or the boiler has exploded or my little brother's gotten himself into trouble and his brakes gave out finally in the Buick and he went plummeting down a ravine, down. And with this strange woman performing on me I would hear the phone ringing far off across our quiet town, ringing as she slithers up and down on me, ringing as she moans and I moan to appease her, thinking of food, and I realize I've abandoned myself, that I lost myself somewhere among this massive piece of fleshy baggage I carry around with me.

I left town, but U stayed. I moved twenty miles away to a little farmhouse where I could live out my fat life, but U moved toward the very center of Venice into a loft in a house overlooking the town square. As I said, I understood his jealousy.

We had all slept with so many of the easy women, so many married women, so many waitresses, so many factory girls, so many other men's women that it was a sheerly logical conclusion, a statistically derived given that someone must be sleeping with Larissa. I wanted to sleep with her myself. Larissa had green eyes.

U had a bad habit of parading her in front of us the first months they were together. He showed her off, telling us in front of her that she had drifted into town (that first night) into Venice with the news that the factory was hiring again, drifted in with the many homeless women who had lost themselves in the middle of the New Depression in the middle of the seventies in the middle of the Midwest, lost themselves in the absurd world, coming to Venice because there was nowhere else to go. He sent her into the bar ahead of him as he made some excuse to stay in the car. Marissa was friendly and I courted her in a joking manner, those first months. She liked me especially because I was so fat, I assumed. Once she confessed to me that she had been fat when she was a little girl, but then, one day, she said, she discovered she was beautiful.

"When was that?" I asked her.

"The day my mother died." She uttered this with such disarming innocence that I heard the pudgy little girl in her saying it, one finger stuck wetly into her mouth. She wore a white cotton blouse and blue slacks that hugged her thighs.

"Can I buy you a drink?" I asked. Her thighs worked against the barstool.

"Sure. But, I'll buy you one back." Her nipple pushed against the sheer material of her blouse, but chastely.

"You know," I told her impulsively, "if you ever want to get away . . ." and I added a little cough, a laugh, "I mean, if you need someone to give you another perspective on things . . . well, I," I broke off.

"Oh thanks, Fat Man," she said with her kindest smile. "Thanks, Darrel." She was the only one who used my given name. I told it to her in a moment of fat weakness, of *largesse.*

And U with his uncanny sense of timing walked in then, smiled indulgently at everybody, shook my hand and ostentatiously rubbed his palm over Cerissa's rump.

So I was surprised when he called me up and told me in a hoarse whisper that he had something important to tell me and that I should hurry over.

Even then, ten years ago, U drank too much. U, you see, was usually reliably drunk. I mean, he was reliably drunk, usually, therefore, usually unreliable. He was, that is, an unreliable narrator and would grow more so as I would ply him with bourbon at the grill or with beer at home and he would tell me, his old buddy, "Fat Man, you got imagination."

How untrue this was. He summoned me to his great loft in his house overlooking the square, made me drive the twenty miles into town, trudge up three flights of ill-lit stairs, and, as though that feat were not enough for my bulk (Oh, how I had grown! I was an expansive soul, grew so large to cushion the pushin' of an unsympathetic world, or to absorb it, bring it inwards; grew so large that the limits of my sight blurred, I grew nearsighted as my cheeks puffed up forcing my eyes to become slits, squeeze shut, and the far edges of my body merged with the fluffy cosmos), I had to climb those stairs and, finally, a narrow ladder that creaked under me and swayed, just so I could get into the loft where U would tell me . . .

U paced in front of me (it took several paces to traverse my front) from smelly brown couch to window to couch again, pausing in his narrative only to fill his glass with sour mash, yelling out at the top of his lungs (When he drank the drink went to his pecker and his voice, and his speech became positively phallic, spewed the great spermatazoan rhetoric of the collapsed grammar of his compulsion). (My parentheses are as fat as I am.) the progeny of his dangerous and pained imagination (If I presume to speak for U, understand, please, that not only did the source lie, manipulate, swagger, stagger, and burp, reel and mutter, stutter, discard, flourish and expand, interpolate, repeat and deny according to the vagaries of his sudden storms of thought, but that it must be admitted when I pretend to present U's material confessions I have already inserted my own taints and details):

"You and me, we're buddies," he began that first night, even before I had finished heaving from the exertion of my climb, "and maybe you were trying to look out for U, but U

wouldn't listen, wouldn't hear, no, U had to be blind, U had to
put his head so far up his ass he couldn't see daylight, couldn't
see his buddies are trying to tell himself something, that
someone else's something was slipping inbetween U's woman's thighs, the bitch! And when I turned off all the lights
and took off all my clothes and lay down on my belly and
looked and waited I SAW!" He screamed these last words.
Complained against that bad act of sight. Vicious voyeurism. I
hadn't unravelled what he meant yet either. From what he
told me, though, it seemed he suspected Teresa of going out
on him.

The first night he suspected her he lay on his belly, naked,
on the hardwood floor with his neck craned up so he could see
out the bottom of the tall window through the venetian blinds
onto the square. U and Felicia never kept furniture near the
windows, so the loft would get as much light as possible. U was
as afraid of getting caught, that first night, spying out of his
own house, of being seen, as he was seeing what he was so
driven to discover. Perhaps more. He lay on his belly for
hours, from three a.m. on, waiting for her to return from her
swing shift at the factory.

"Wasn't that painful?" I asked him.

"Didn't notice. Oh, I did, but didn't want to, the pain was
good for me, kept me alert . . ."

Because all the roads in Venice lead into the square, and
the one she would approach on spills its main traffic parallel
to the line of sight from U's window, U couldn't anticipate
when Denise would return by, for instance, staring out the
window down the long street watching for headlamps.
Instead, he had to press his face to the window, crane his neck
and strain his eyes sideways and down, looking down his nose
and cheeks, holding his breath so that the windows would not
fog up, trying to discern the slight incremental growth of light
(or perhaps, the indistinguishable diminutions in the shadow
of the square), trying to detect the approach of a car, straining
his hearing to the sounds of a car coming. Every distant
whoosh excited him. Every slight dilation of his pupils was

confused for the growing light signalling the approach of his lover. This incredible effort sustained over the weary hours before dawn was killing.

The cars passed through town infrequently at that hour. Most of U's time was filled with awfulnesses. His thoughts rushed as madly as his speeches did to me then, in his loft, obsessively, inexorably, suddenly, like an electric current running through a jerking frog's muscle. Incapable of reflection he was reduced to reflex. Incapable of maintaining his objectivity, here, naked, on the hardwood floor, he became subject to his own excruciating experiments in jealousy. In lucid moments he might have noted with a sneering irony to what extent the human organism is capable of tormenting itself. Perhaps not. In any case, I digress.

At first the sound of tire on asphalt competed with the blood thudding in his ears. But he soon became expert at judging by these sounds whether the car was slowing or accelerating, whether it had caught the red light forty yards down the street on which his lover was expected to arrive, or whether it was coming from one of the many other roads which led into the square. Finally, as cars on the road were heard approaching the intersection, U would hunker down further, pressing his thighs and belly against a now-warm floor, (in the same position a bored but polite husband would assume during copulation with his wife, on his elbows). He muttered to himself a secret incantation and lowered the venetian blind so that the last yellow slat fell just above the windowsill and he could peer above it, through the narrow slit, onto the square.

"I was sure every goddamned car was hers. And I was just as sure that the next one was hers too, as soon as the first one passed by."

The second night of his vigil he learned that the headlights of the cars as they approached on Backside Drive were reflected in the windows of the house across the other side of the square. Because of the angle of intersection and the gentle declination of Backside Drive as it entered the square, the lights shone in the last window to the left on the second floor of the house across the street and reflected into the middle window of the fourth floor of U's house. This was feasible. I checked. As U ranted on I casually went over to that middle window and soon substantiated that a definite reflected glow growing into a harsh yellow glare preceded an automobile into the square.

U's days soon began to empty themselves of color as his nighttime ritual became harder and harder a habit to break. His days were haunted by the fixed image of a colorless street brushed by the shadows of a leafless tree waving in front of the street lamp in the center of the little grassy mall in the square. At random and uncontrollable moments, the reflected glare of headlights in a window would flash across his diurnal brain, searing a message of obsession and blinding him. During long crescendos in drum solos on the radio he could discern the terrible nocturnal whisper of tires rubbing along asphalt. U found himself wandering over to the window even when Clarissa was home, experiencing the same, though muted, wistfulness that he felt in the minutes between nighttime cars, a vagueness played in minor keys.

The maniacal fixedness of U's stares at the crucial window across the street was not an empty one. Far from it. U filled those uncomfortable hours with fantasies—rather, one should say, with *a* fantasy, a scene—that he replayed over and over again. This scene, of Alicia's arrival, was edited and sculpted until it was honed to its uttermost cruelty. Over and over again, U tortured himself with the image of Marissa arriving home in a bartender's car. You see, he was sure that she was cheating on him with the bartender of a grill across the street from her factory. This bartender, however, was an affable sort of fellow. Once, out of curiosity, I went to the grill to see if he was really there, if there was in fact even a grill across from the factory, or if these were just genies conjured by U's mental rubbings. He was real, and his bar, too. He was not Teresa's type, if I may say so. Though U wasn't her type either. That's another story however,

43

". . . arriving home in this fellow's car and reaching over for him as they stopped in front of my house, reaching for him and dragging him, his head to hers and, and, in an unbelievable, I . . ."

And in an unbelievable accident of light, with a wave of a certain branch away from the streetlight, there would be a sudden illumination, and U could see her lips gleaming, her eyes closed, her body yielding to the pressure, his hands gliding over her belly, her thighs, her breasts.

"And, and . . ."

And in a similar accident of sound the wind would suddenly shift and though it was winter and the windows rolled up U could hear the words, confused perhaps in the rustling of dry branches which hung over the street and slapped against the sides of his house.

" 'I hate to go in,' Melissa would say. 'I could stay here all night.'

" 'Listen, Liss,' ("I hated that," U said, " especially that 'Liss.' She always insisted I call her by her whole name."), 'listen, Liss, we gotta keep things cool until we can work something out.'

"Yes, and, and . . ."

But these auditory and visual hallucinations always enjoyed a clarity that her real homecomings lacked. Melinda would arrive, yes, sometimes in a big car, but always that of another factory girl, one who had, perhaps, found herself a sugar daddy. Anyway, it didn't make much of a difference. U felt too guilty to look long or hard at her arrival; he would never take more than a half-second's glance, afraid of getting caught, before bobbing his head below the window.

Then, as Belinda said goodnight to her lift and tiredly mounted the stairs, he would rush, naked, on tip-toes through the darkened loft to their broad bed and pretend to be asleep as she entered, quickly undressed and slipped into the still-cold bed with him. "Mmm," he would mumble into his pillow, though she was usually asleep, already, at last unaware, innocent.

"Every time a car would pass I would say to myself, 'U, forget that Bitch. She's wasted enough of your time. One more car,' I'd say, you see they'd usually come every five or ten minutes at that hour in the morning, I mean, like who the hell drives around in this town at that hour? and so I'd say to myself, 'One more car, pussyligger' as though I had one part kickin' another part in the head, in my head, telling it to Get Straight (he would shout these slogans at me), GET STRAIGHT, like a drug was going through my veins and I wanted to get clean of it, get back to my real work, but the junkie in me couldn't and I'd say, 'One more car,' and the last car would approach and I'd hunker down, it would catch the light at the top of the hill, finally pass by, and I'd be watching the window across the street and I'd say 'This is the one, she's in this one,' but then it would pass and I'd still be there, couldn't resist the temptation to stay there, left flat, man, on my belly, losing. So I'd stay, telling myself, 'This is the last one,' like an idiot rehearsing his name over and over again and forgetting it. What's your name? Uhhhhh.

"Until I realized I was defeated by the whole game, and I'd really decide to go to bed after the next car, and then, oh man, one wouldn't come for half an hour and my resolve would be wiped out but worse, I felt much worse, because I realized that the world is unpredictable and, and terrible, that it works in a string of accidents and the goddamned universe was designed to make men crazed, superstitious, believe in ghosts and worshippers of nothing, much worse than, than no car, much worse was a string of cars, in the middle of the night at four a.m., three, five, ten even in a row, one after the other; whooooom, whoooom, whooooom, whooooom, bumper to bumper like RUSH HOUR (another slogan) after twenty minutes of nothing and after I was just getting those feeling of SOLE SURVIVALISM, (he was a repository of slogans, neon signs that would flash on and off in his head. He was the pure passionate product of America; he thought in ungrammatical fragments; his rhetoric was a disarray of BOLD LETTERS) of LAST MAN ON EARTHISM, and then this accident, ten of them, a decoincidence, and I felt, if I could somehow predict when a string would hit like that, well, if I could, then, well, I don't known, I could break the bank."

(He was hiding something, he became silent, fell into a frustrated boggy silence.)

"Well, it would at least be ENTERTAINING! Yes," (his eyes lit up with the grace of insight), "you see," (he ambled over to me, grabbing me by my shirt lapels as I sat quietly sipping beer and munching on pretzels, and whispered at me in a ludicrous stage whisper as though we were conspirators), "you see man, I wasn't, uh, *Jealous,* I was bored, man, bored to the ends of my nerves, to the rattail ragged EDGES OF MY NEUTRONS, to the AXED CONNECTIONS OF MY AXONS, to the very DEAD ENDS OF MY DENDRITES, bored, empty, scared, lonely, wanted to stay high and buzz, babe, but alone, bored, and then, then . . ."

Then he would start predicting the next car, counting to a certain number, slowly, teasing himself, and in this moments telling himself, "Fifty-nine. The next car's gonna come when I count to fifty-nine," and he told me he felt like he knew, for certain, when they would come, trying not to cheat, because he was right, he felt clairvoyant, and telekinetic, like he could influence the arrivals. It made his belly-life richer and he was high priest of that world, "A GODDAMED ORACLE," he told me, "I not only knew what was gonna happen I made it happen."

During one of these sessions, U confessed, he began to look forward to these nights on his belly. "Man, I'd lay there naked, and if it was warm enough, unable to read or think or nap, oh I'd try to nap but it would kill me, KILL ME that I didn't know when she'd be coming home, I mean, I didn't know what she was doing! And then I'd think about her coming home in the car and my cock would get hard like this . . ."

He rushed over to me and pushed his fist in my face. He had an enormous forearm and he grabbed it with his other hand holding it all a-quiver with the red knot of flesh at the end and I could imagine U's horse's cock creeping between his body and the wood floor, creeping and growing toward the window, seeking his lost Charisse.

"And I'd get hard like this and then roll and push and think, stopping if I heard a car coming or saw headlights in the window, holding my breath and keeping perfectly still, yes, that would make my head spin and my . . . I'd start feeling better but, . . . and cars passed and for half a moment I would rub and rub again until I felt I couldn't keep myself back any more and then I'd rock into a crouching position and sit back on my heels and hold the window open for a blast of air striking my pecker hard like hand's touch and push it out the window rub more and it would shake up and down between the window and the window sill rattling until I'd let go my whole uh . . . KARMA, yeah, spraying it over the trees, over the lawn, out onto the street, until it fell like rain on the cars, on all the cars, on the cars with my Priscilla, on hers too so she would understand, though she never did, understand my heat, coming to tell you, Prissy . . . coming home, come on, baby, come on home, come . . ."

"Did you do this every night, U?" I asked him.

"Oh, man, I yeah, I did *this*," (he mocked my fastidiousness), "twice and three times a night, but always, every night, naked."

"Out of boredom, U?"

"You don't understand very much, do you buddy?" He turned away and paced silently up and down the room while I sat on his brown couch a few more polite minutes before putting on my jacket (I was too large to wear a regular jacket. My aunt made me this one out of a horse blanket), and nodding silently to my possessed host, I climbed down the ladder, down the three flights of stairs, got into my car and drove the twenty miles home, occasionally washing my windshield just to be sure.

Of course, I couldn't very well go all the way home without eating something, so I stopped at the Pizzeria a couple of miles outside town and ordered a large one to go with extra cheese and mushrooms, pepperoni and onions. The counter girl told me it would be fifteen minutes, and I decided to while away the time by going out to the parking lot (it was hardly a parking lot, it was just a bare piece of earth where innumerable cars had come for generations so that the younger boys and girls in them could get to know each other a bit better). Funny, something about it still made me want to chuckle, so I leaned against my car, a few yards away from the rest and, munching on a pickle I had bought to tide me over until the pizza was ready, I surveyed the lot of cars with steamed-up windows, cars which rocked up and down and side to side, some of them blaring radio stations, enough of them blaring the one station which played all the top 40 hits so that the lot was transformed into one grand receiver, the cars jigging around, dancing to the music. It was then, in some terrible accident of light, that I saw a familiar head through the side window of a car not too far away rear up on its neck and bend back in the back seat, the face strained and open in an eternal pose of compliance, of surrender, the neck bared in a gesture like the one a victim makes, the face innocent and mild and yet, at the same time, erotically lost, excited, gone in a wild mask of pleasure, smiling—no, baring its teeth, the face the face of Larissa.

I almost dropped the half-eaten pickle and stared and thought that the face nodded at me, though I was upside down to it. I looked around the lot, pretending not to see, but then was forced to look again, and when I turned away I saw that there were faces hung back and lost in excitement staring at me from all the side windows of the back seats of all the cars, and on top of them, faces of men, leering and unconscious, and in all the cars jigging and bouncing were the faithless Larissas and Marissas and Cerissas and Felicias and Denises, Clarissas, Alicias, Teresas, Marisas, Melissas, Belindas, Melindas, and all of them, outside Venice, somewhat blind, though not as blind as poor U, whom I understood best of all.

THE MISOGYNIST

I didn't know what made me get up and come to this
typewriter that first night. Perhaps it was the heat. The night
was muggy, and the two bodies in my bed were heat
generators, could have warmed the entire house in winter, the
sheets were burning up, wet, steaming, we slid into each other
rolling into union on waves of sweat, collapsing in a panting
stupor . . . too hot to sleep, staring dully at the ceiling, perhaps
drifting off in a troubled way for a moment only to be
awakened by an aching thirst. Finally, my wife slept, her body
cooled a bit, though she still breathed like a bitch in an August
afternoon.

So I got up and came to my typewriter. Put a piece of
paper in the roll and began to write some nonsense verse and
then a small voice, not a squeak, more a moan, a low
expression of pain, came from between my legs. I thought it
was the heat and instinctively looked over to my wife, who I
thought was probably dreaming. On hot nights women talk in
their sleep. Listen to them some time, you might learn
something.

"Here, here, here . . ." It was the same voice only a little more distinct coming from between my legs. This time I thought that perhaps it was a mouse chirping, and I shivered despite the heat. Having always been afraid of little creatures; mice and spiders and bats and even mechanical dolls, sometimes frighteningly real, would scare me out of my wits. I lifted my feet off the floor and rolled up a newspaper that was lying on the desk, pushed my chair away from the desk and looked at the floor between my legs, but nothing was there. I returned to typing, thought for a moment that the voice had come from my pants. What would it be like if a cock suddenly found its voice? The thought left me pale and upset. I reached for the paper already in the 'writer and with a shaking hand put a clean one in, began again:

THE MISOGYNIST

by
Roderick Courtship

Perhaps his penis began talking to him in his dreams. He wasn't at all obsessed with his penis. In fact, he tended to ignore it. But like every other lover, he gave his pecker a little name, a diminutive, "Mike," he called it. He had been speaking to it for years, coaxing his Mike, talking into it with its pole and knobby pick-up, coaxingly, lovingly, admonishingly, "This is another fine mess you've got me into." Or, "Mike, I've been counting on you, so don't let me down." Of course, he was just showing off at first, would save these conversations for the co-eds when he was in college. But after his first wife left him he started talking to it when he was alone. Nothing else between them, you understand, just talking into it, sort of recording his thoughts:

"Sure, I know I miss her, but after all, isn't it all for the better? It's just as well; she would have run off sooner or later, we were mismatched. Can't keep a woman like that. Too darn expensive. Emotionally expensive. Had some pretty darn funny habits, too, I'll tell you, they could wear a man down. Like the things she did with rubber hoses. And she would always bend down to rub hunchbacks and pat dwarves on the head. Oh, I know. You're probably wondering how many dwarves and hunchbacks we'd meet. But you'd be surprised. She attracted them. My god! This is the twentieth century, after all! I'd take her to parties and she'd disappear. Come back hours later when the affair was fizzling out and say, 'Oh, dear, I've had such a marvelous time, don't know where the evening's gone!'"

Of course, Desmond only spoke to his little man in the most proper of terms. Desmond had respect for his body, jogged every day, kept himself in shape, though he had forgotten what for. Then, one evening, after his lonely tuna salad dinner by candlelight, Mike started talking back.

"Hey Des. Des! . . .Des!"

"Mike? Is that you, Mike? Are you talking to me?"

"You bet I'm talkin', buddy. Listen, Mo, it's gettin' pretty lonely down here. Whattya say you and me go beaver trappin', y'known what I mean. How about you and me catch us some snatch? How's that sound, buddy?"

"Uh, gee, Mike. I don't know what to say."

"You don't have to say anything, Jackson . . . I'll do all the talkin'. In fact, maybe you could start gettin' used to it, because now I got my yapper workin' it's gonna be hard to stop. Now will ya let me out of here?" Desmond still had his pecker caught in his pants. Somewhat bewildered, he quickly unzipped his fly and with some difficulty produced Mike, who was rampant and throbbing, though Desmond had not touched him. Mike began jabbering as soon as he was out . . .

My wife rolled on our bed, moaning again, "Mi . . . My . . . Oh, my . . .!" an erotic, salcious quiver in her thighs, bared to the humid night as I wrote.

. . . his mouth working in soft "plups" of his lips, adding a sort of wetness to his words that made everything sound as though it were spoken with a leer.

"Now, listen, bro'. Since it's my birthday, why don't you take me out on the town? You can get on one of those leisure suits, you know, maybe that green one you wore to your old lady's wedding . . . Goddamn, she was a fine piece of ass she was . . . but you blew it, couldn't hold on to the bitch. I was holding up my end, so to speak, but you couldn't follow through. That was always your problem, no follow through. And you swallowed all the women's lib crap too, lapped it up. Little lap dog Desmond. All ya had to do was slap her around a little. Anyway, we're not going to make those mistakes again. This time, I'm in charge."

"Now, you look here, Mike. You can't expect to take over. I can't believe this. This is absurd. I'm sitting here talking to my own . . . I'm *arguing* with my own penis, and it's, he's talking back. I must be out of my mind." Desmond appealed to some unseen audience.

Mike quivered in front of Desmond and squinted at him somewhat maliciously, if one could imagine that the eye of a penis head screwing up could be called a squint. It then throbbed more and more, quivering like a divining rod trying to tune in to those vibrations that signalled water was nearby, like a divining rod using the diviner as an instrument instead of a guiding intelligence. A low grunt of pleasure escaped from Desmond. He bit his lips and rolled his head back, his hands twitching at his side.

"Hey, mmmf . . . cut that out."

"What's wrong, Don't you like it?" There was a strange cool, self-possession in Mike's voice. A dangerous threat.

"Come off it now, will you please. I like it. I like it. Oh, gee, c'mon, man."

"You're even beginning to talk like me, friend."

"I'll do anything you say."

"Take me out tonight."

"O.K. O.K. Just don't make me come, no, make me . . ."

"It's been so long
Since I got held by you
I'm gettin' mean and lonely
And I'm always blue . . ." Mike sang, little bubbles frothing on the lips of his mouth.

"It has been sort of a long time, hasn't it?"

"You bet, momma."

"I guess it couldn't hurt."

"Listen to this guy."

"Let's go."

"Whooooeeeee!" The pecker whistled, a rusty whistle more like a squeaking hiss as it expelled air through its nose/mouth/eye. This virgin whistle surprised Desmond, who muttered, "Just what I needed, a whistling prick."

The writing was so simplistic, so colloquial, so pedestrian it hurt me. There is an actual pain, an inner rash that is irritated and can't be relieved when you're creating something so bad it hurts but you know you must continue, see the thing through, this awful crisis of confidence, this failure of nerve. Perhaps some writers come to welcome this awful itch, and masochistically plunge into drivel as they would into a warm bath with slit wrists. I tried to change my tack slightly, but I knew I would never be the writer I aspired to be.

Mike spoke to Desmond all the way to the bar.
". . . and remember that night you won big at poker and we walked into the biggest cathouse in Berlin and went right up to that big blonde, that tall glass of milk, oh man, I still get hard when I think of that lassie, oh colleen, you little squash pie, you.
You let me in the . . ."
"Mike, I was a conscientious objector. I worked years to get that C.O.. I keep on telling you I never was in the army."
". . . *in the front door*
You went up and down and down
Then you let me in the back door
Where the devil was so brown.
I laughed and shook my head . . ."
"Hey, that's against the law," Desmond objected.
"You tried to push me out
I pointed at the bed
Achtung mein kinde Kraut."
Desmond pulled the car into a large parking lot across the street from a place he once heard his colleagues mention. He taught in a suburban high school, kept to himself. But one day he heard a gym teacher before a faculty meeting tell the story of how he met his fiancée. It was at the Back Door Inn; Desmond resolved to try it.
The Back Door Inn was a converted warehouse. Its entire front had been bricked up, two stories high and fifty yards

across. It seemed to be flush with the building next to it, and the enormity of its blankness dwarfed the couples and single men and women who walked in front of it. As Desmond approached the wall it loomed up to overwhelm his sense; the purposeless wall was a false front, a mural depicting nothing but itself, a self-reflexive text on silence, meaninglessness. It was poorly lit, so the small foot path between the Inn and that building next door (a bank, Desmond noticed) couldn't be seen until he actually stood next to it and saw two disembodied fluorescent breasts lying on the ground on either side of the narrow alleyway into which people seemed literally to be swallowed. The trickle of people was engorged between the lit tits, which then seemed to Desmond more like two canine teeth. He joined them, stepping with a certain trepidation into the narrow defile. He was forced to hold the sides of the walls next to him because of the intense disorienting gloom. He stepped as quickly as he could, frightened by the ghostly whispers that echoed along the bottom of the chasm. The slightest sound reverberated back and forth until it was magnified; the partyers in the single file fell silent, trying to diminish the funereal effect, then scared themselves into hysterical laughter distorted into a horrifying cacaphony by the acoustics of the pathway.

The walls curved slightly, and the path descended in an almost imperceptible decline. Sensation was reduced to a minimum; whoever had designed the place found the threshhold levels—skin temperature, odorlessness, the barest of light ambient in even darkness—and maintained the conditions there, at the limen of human perception. No sense or design could be determined from the information Desmond's eyes, ears or fingers gave him. The walls were heated by inner coils to body temperature; the air along the corridor was still but not stifling. Desmond began to think of himself as a passive projectile forced into some emission, travelling down this tube to some forbidden and strange fruit.

"Hey, what the hell's going on out there? Get me out of here." Mike's words came muffled out of Desmond's pants. The woman just in front of him turned around to stare at him as though he were some sort of cowardly novice. Desmond let go of the wall with one hand to hold his crotch.

"I can't see. It's dark as poozle in here," Mike insisted.

The defile spewed suddenly into a large cavern: LIGHTS FLASHED all around in bursts that blinded, spelling incomprehensible words from below and above in all the gaudy colors of psycheindelicacy. An assault of sound pounded the body; the bass line throb reverberated in the chests of the tube travellers newly-arrived, a throb so loud it controlled the beat of their hearts, forced that muscle into sympathetic vibration, pulsation, made breathing difficult. And then the fetid smell, so overwhelming, of locker rooms, of semen, of dripping genitals and cheap perfume, of cigarette smoke, of stale booze breathed doubly, of shoe polish and raw leather and wet wool and underarm deodorant and shit and puke and greasy hamburger, of skin rotting and of the raw wound of pustulous, acned faces, a smell so overwhelming it invaded the other senses and confused the electrochemical bath between nerves in the brain, the serotonin bubbling, broiling and burping, confusing and crossfiring and shorting out and soon one could see the smells and hear the bursts of purple light on the retina as bells, and smell the white noise of the ultra-amplified music as an oxish musk, and in this fertile moment the brain was brought to revelation . . .

"I got to get out of here. I must leave this place," Desmond mumbled.

"Hey, chief, relax. We just got started, Sam. I can just smell all that muff out there."

"I've got to get out of here," Desmond insisted, dubious.

"Listen. One drink at the bar, babe, and we'll leave."

"Now. I want to leave now." Desmond stood rooted, rigid.

"One drink, old man. You promised."

Desmond forced his way against the brutal flood of people and sensation and entered the Back Door. Two giant oblate rubber globes guarded either side. On one, someone had scrawled in pink lipstick:

> LET GO YOUR HOPE
> OH SIMPLE DOPE.
> IN YOU GO
> TO JOIN THE SHOW.

Desmond heard whinnies, screams and sirens.
Desmond saw vaguely a group of disembodied heads

floating in a line. When one face brought a glass to its lips, he realized the heads were connected to bodies sitting around a bar.

"*I got my tale-teller tellin,*" Mike sang.

"*tattlin' a tale,*
gonna score big,
know it can't fail."

"That's pretty weak stuff, Mike," Desmond said. He was cheered by the crowd of young women who seemed to dominate the place. "You were better off whistling."

There was only one empty seat at the bar, next to a child-woman with wild blonde hair and a halter top that jiggled every time she moved, which was constantly, her ass squirming on the tiny barstool. These maneuvers were meant to distract onlookers from her face, a pitted and smelly affair. Desmond was somewhat intimidated by the ongoing show her body staged, but he sat next to her anyway. He ordered a scotch and soda and tried to tune it all out. He was determined to keep his mouth shut, finish his drink and leave, but Mike was just as determined.

"Who are we sitting next to, Des?"

"Blonde."

"Hubba, hubba!"

"Oh, shut up."

The blonde heard Desmond's part of this interchange, thought to herself: another damned kook. She had always attracted kooks, pervs, soliloquizing alkies, junkies. She smelt like the dickens. Desmond realized that he was, essentially, talking to himself and looked around in complete mortification. Smiling weakly at the woman and nodding, he renewed his vow of silence.

"Hey, Blondie!" Mike literally shouted. "Hey, Cutie-pie, I like your smile." She wasn't smiling. She (Was she seventeen? Twenty-seven? Thirty-seven?) turned around but couldn't see her suitor. Only the guy with the glasses next to her who sat with the same sinking, sickly smile.

"Whattya say we make hay, Faye?"

She turned around quickly this time, trying to catch the loser next to her in the act. Desmond only shrugged his shoulders and rolled his eyes up at the ceiling in a gesture of innocence. She continued to stare at him as Mike yelled.

"C'mon momma, don't be shy!"

Desmond clapped his hand over his mouth and shook his head violently. It dawned on the woman that the unassuming schmuck next to her was a ventriloquist, and a smile of appreciation cracked her pitted face.

"You're pretty good. Do that again."

"Ooooh, alright! I got something here you want to see."

Desmond blushed.

"C'mon," the woman laughed. "That's fantastic. Don't be modest. You're great!"

"You're not bad yourself," Mike shouted.

Desmond took a large gulp of his drink to show he couldn't possibly be speaking, pointing with one hand at his mouth, a dribble of scotch leaking from the corner.

"Jesus," she said. "I've never seen one so good. God, you're *good!*" She rubbed her leg up and down Desmond's thigh and put her skinny hand on his arm, squeezing it.

"I get better."

"Let's see."

"Let's go," Mike said.

"Miss, I am *not* a ventriloquist," Desmond said at the same time.

The woman's face lit up and she clapped her hands in childish glee.

I had been typing furiously, oblivious to the typos and epos, just having some distracted fun on a hot evening, trying to forget about the heat or my wife's thighs. The story, I realized, was rather silly, but it might have implications; sort of a pornographic parable, an anatomical Gogolian absurdity, or so I comforted myself. These meditations were interrupted by the feeling of a warm suffusion on the inside of my thigh followed by a strange rub in my crotch. I thought I had gotten hard as might happen when I would get lost in directionless revery, and it was pushing against the open drawer of my desk.

"Hey, you! Hey! Allo? Allo?"

I closed my eyes and laughed, realized that it was three or four in the morning, it was hot, I was tired and I had been writing so quickly that I had mesmerized myself into a sort of hyperimaginative state. My story about the talking pecker was more naturalistic than my usual stuff, and though the premise was absurd, I had imagined real characters had truly participated in the story. But then I felt the tug at my own pecker and heard the voice again, my auto-suggested voice.

"Let me out of here please, mister."

I groaned. I tried to remember the number of my psychoanalyst, but realized I didn't have a psychoanalyst, that only characters in my stories do. I leaned away from the desk and opened the flap of my pyjamas.

A tiny woman three inches tall put her arms on each thigh and lifted herself up through the material. She was entirely naked and looked like she stepped out of an advertisement for prophylactics in a European magazine.

"Oh ya, it is stuffy in there. Whew."

"Oh, shit." I felt dizzy, but decided to ride this one out.

"What do you mean by this 'oh shit'? Is this the way you talk to the ladies?"

"Oh, hell, . . . I mean, I apologize, but . . ."

"Oh, ha, ha," the little creature laughed, the sound tiny enough to break my wondering heart. Precious, precious, I had conjured a little gem. "It is all right. To this I am accustomed."

"Well, I am sorry."

"So? Who are you, big man? You wear such funny clothings."

She had perched herself on the lip of my pyjama fly and was swaying on the taut material. She examined her nails carefully, or so I thought. I could not see her nails. Her fingers were sliver-small.

"What do you mean, who am I? Who are you? How did you get in there anyway?" I asked her.

"I do not know, and I do not care. It was nice in there." She looked at me slyly.

"You're French, aren't you?"

"But of course, silly man. You Americans are so provincial."

I couldn't stand looking at her nakedness. Her body was perfectly formed in every detail, and I traced the curve of her thighs and breasts and neck and looked at the reddish bush at the V of her thighs and could even see that her nipples were hard, her skin gleamed. An erection, I noticed with horror, was mounting uncontrollably toward my little friend and was about to push her off her perch on the fabric of my pyjamas. I gently lifted her up and put her on my typewriter, facing me. She crossed her legs, sitting on the 'F' key.

"Rod? Rod, honey? Who are you talking to?" My wife stirred in our bed but kept her eyes closed.

"Nobody, love. Go back to sleep. I'm just trying out some dialogue in this story I'm working on. Go back to sleep."

"Who is that lady?" the little woman wanted to know.

She looked at me in puzzlement, the features expressing her confusion somehow recognizably despite the miniature rendition. "An old American joke," I said. "I guess you wouldn't understand. C'est ma femme. M'épouse. Her name is . . ."

"You did not ask me *my* name."

It hadn't occurred to me that hallucinations had names. I was still less than convinced I wasn't completely out of my bird. "O.K.," I sighed. "What's your name?"

"Minette."

"Pleased to meet you, Minette." I held the corner of my pinky to her and she took it in between her two hands. Then I tore a corner from a tissue and asked her to wrap herself.

"What's the matter. Is there something wrong with the way I look?"

"Not at all, Minette. Please don't misunderstand." God. Not only was she small, but she was sensitive, too. Not only was she sensitive, but she was seductive. God, I thought, I'm telling my own fantasy to cover up because she tempts me too much. Tempts me to do what, though? That's what I'd like to know, I thought. What is it she tempts me to do? This strange attitude could only come from gazing too long and too hard at miniature naked women in girlie magazines as a boy, and yes, as a man: in barber shops ('Hey, sonny, that one's not for you. Why don't you read the new Jimmy Olson? Got a new Jimmy Olson just this week. Over there. That's right. Now why don't you put that down like a good boy,' while the lathered and steaming face under his razor guffawed and the lather bobbled and bib shook); under the porch, propped against garbage cans in alleyways, casually in waiting rooms, chewing harder at the piece of gum, working the jaw to appease the joint in these public places; yes. Oh, you miniature ladies! Oh you three-inch high images of spilt-seed love and spit and sweat throb and beat hum rub drum and jerk spit sigh roll eyes, roll chew jaw working oh joint! jacking it up higher and up and yes oh yes, I loved you all, little ladies, in my o(w)nanistic way.

And now. What was it she tempted me to do? Three inches high and French. Oh tacky dream! Oh shlock incarnation of middle American hope! My Minette.

I spoke to her well into the night and past the dawn. My wife slept soundly, especially in the cooler hours before the dawn. Minette told me the last thing she remembered was falling asleep next to her boyfriend, that she and her boyfriend were going to be married in April. It sounded to me like another dull European alliance, contracted out of necessity and boredom and ineluctable social constraints. All that time I pondered the simple wishful moments in my lascivious past that might have been brought to realization, and then the long wistful moments produced by the marriage which was the realization of one of those simple wishful moments. A bad marriage. No, not a bad marriage. Rather, a terrible, a disastrous, a pitiable and drunken eleven-year shouting contest, an emotional street brawl without shame or reservation, a psychological blitzkrieg that we played out in such fervor that it would make even the stoniest-hearted man collapse and break down in a howl of hystrical laughter. And now, this Minette.

"Ah, my boyfriend, he is such a brute. He does nothing except complain about the government. He cannot work of course. He spends all his time drinking and complaining."

"Why don't you leave him, then," I said selfishly.

"Why, it looks as though I have done this already, no?"

For a reason I did not yet fully understand, this made me exultantly happy. This infelicity on her part, the half-pledge of an as-yet-unspoken allegiance, made me hopeful. Still, the idea was a ridiculous one; I recoiled at the thought of taking Minette as a mistress.

But why shouldn't I? Why the hell not? After all, I reasoned, she was perfect, a perfect woman. (1) She only incompletely understood my language and, (2) She only a quarter heard what she did not understand. This was the most important factor in her perfection. I could say to her . . . anything, and she would only blink. Americanisms and euphemisms were lost on her. It gave me a privacy greater than any that could be created by walls or costumes. I could hide in my own language. (3) She was bite-size. Her smallness made her anonymous, controllable, unthreatening. Her worst furies and resentments would seem no more than tempests in a teapot, something less than comic. (4) She was an unregistered alien, and had no identity other than that which I granted her, no more than if she were precisely a product of my own fancy. (5) She could be supported without any work at all. One of my meals could satisfy her for a decade. (6) She would be slavishly dedicated to me, dependent on me. In the end, at bottom yes, this must be considered, too: (7) I could merely crush her between thumb and forefinger if she got out of hand. The perfect muder. Her body could be thrown into the Dispos*All automatic garbage crusher. She would not be missed in this hemisphere. Her boyfriend had probably already forgotten her, found some other.

These considerations were no different in style than those conjured by all the other times I had met a woman for the first time and, though only a few moments had passed between us, I was already calculating feverishly, summing and deciding, trying to weave her into some pragmatic fantasy, testing her looks, her tastes, her ideas, the qualities of her mind, her viability as a potential mate. The considerations this time were no different, the process no more abstract nor more emotional, only more extreme. I had already, in my head, divorced my wife, divided the property, quit my job, moved into a home with her, bought toy furniture, perhaps even the antique kind perfect in every detail, like her, French, Louis Quatorze beds and Henri Cinq sofas, toys created for the children of French aristocracy. We would of course move out of the city: too many people, too many spying eyes, too many places to get lost in, to lose her in. (Yet, I wondered if my jaded fellow city dwellers would blink of they saw Minette, or would they think her just another commercial ploy, an advertisement for a coming movie, even forget about her when advertisements failed to appear . . .) I'd get lost with her in exurbia, among wide lawns and high hedges, my self and my adoring, faithful, captive, little Gallic hearthrob.

Of course there were obvious difficulties. Some of them have probably occurred to you. They need not be enumerated. But if you think about them for a horny week or two, you too will find a solution as satisfying as ours, a mutually fulfilling expression of commingled lust and love. A hint: it was all done with mirrors. Funhouse mirrors.

All, all of that initial fantasy came to pass: the country cottage, the divorce (a simple procedure, my wife had been expecting it for a long time. She told the judge that she thought being married to a writer, when she was young, would be somehow different. She was experimenting, out of inertia, out of ennui, out of a mild bemusement at my passion. Oh yes, I had courted her passionately. But unless you think it is in my character to court passionately but tire quickly of newborn love, read on.) All came to pass except the murder, except the daring, delicious crush between thumb and forefinger, the dispatch of a tiresome toy to toy-heaven. No. Not that. Could I have been so cruel? Was I so cruel that I could even have conceived the crime? Oh, but I am a profound misogynist! I had a Desmond's Mike inside me, too. In fact, of all my characters, Mike is most like me. No, not the specious writer, the divorced sentimentalist, the passionate, infinitely needy most desirous mask of a mask. But there is a self which haunts the self, the doppelganger mirror to deep unutterable plottings, a less articulate self which gazes at a grotesque, a worst-of-all-possible life as benignly and as hauntingly as the eye of a penis. And there lay my lurking inner Mike, recording and amplifying.

A year later, after Minette first popped out of my fly and after I wrote the first part of "The Misogynist," I found that I could take the story somewhere. The matters which had occupied me all that year no longer mattered, no longer dominated my life.

Mike's initial success frightened Desmond, who was brought up to believe that nice guys at least finished, and therefore he was the sort of man who went through life more or less losing, suffering through his losses, becoming happy at losing until he finally discovers that his losses are victories. The pecker, however, was more interested in tying, in meeting the world head on, at least the world of sex. Desmond found that he and Mike had little to say to each other. Mike was more smooth, more interested in the process than finalities. Mike could not understand why Desmond always acted and talked like his life was almost over.

Mike controlled Desmond's night life through his glandular manipulations, but Desmond retreated to his day, his work. He taught social studies in a suburban high school. One day, about a year after Mike's 'birthday' the two intelligences greeted each other, Desmond with a precaffeinated grumble, Mike with an erectile, gaping head and leering mouth. Over coffee, Mike spoke.

"Listen, Desmond. What do ya say before you put me away we skip schooldaze today and hit the streets. Like man, I'm tired of that ventriloquist routine."

"Now Mike, we've been through this before. The nights…"

". . . are yours and the days are mine," Mike mocked.

"Mike, I'd be lying if I said I didn't enjoy our nights, and well, I've learned some things, too. But enough is enough, don't you think, old friend? All work and no play, you know what I mean, Mike?"

"Hey, now, Tonto. Do you think what I do ain't work? I sweat my balls off trying to get you laid, and you, you turkey, tell me that we're just jerking off."

"Well, I'm not going to quibble with you. If I don't work you don't get to, either."

"Prissy bastard."

"Name calling again."

"Shitfay, Mothafug. Cogsug. Catshit slig reamer . . ."

"I'm putting you away."

". . . pussylig, pigfug, asslig . . ."

"Polymorphous pervert! Generalissimo Genitalis!"

"Okay, wiseass," Mike muttered as Desmond forced him back into his pants. "We'll see who puts who away."

"And just what do you mean by that threat?"

In school, Mike was good through homeroom. Desmond sat down most of the time during homeroom, anyway. But during first period, Desmond strode into class with a provocative bulge in the front of his pants. Mike entered the class ten inches in front of Desmond and greeted the class through the fabric of Desmond's pants.

"Hey, boys and girls! Let's get it on!"

Neither the class nor Desmond could register what they heard. Desmond stood stock still a few feet inside the classroom, blushing and speechless, hoping the class hadn't heard. The students looked around the room to see who had shouted out of turn. Desmond considered bluffing his way through it and started to demand, in the most authoritative voice he could muster: "O.K. Who's got the tape recorder . . ." but then Sylvia Petrazynski, who had just transferred from parochial school, screamed, clapped her hand over her eyes, pointed at Mr. Smickel's pants and propelled her one hundred and eighty pounds out the door. The class watched in silence as Mike, pounding against the krylon zipper of Desmond's pants, managed to stick his head out and confronted the class.

"Excuse me, kiddies," he said. In an orderly but spontaneous rush the entire class filed out of the room, in their native and self-conscious embarrassment trying not to look at Mr. Smickel, everyone blushing except for Desmond, who wept silently in his place in the front of the room. In the next few moments left him he grabbed Mike around the neck and began to squeeze, hoping to choke the little man to death, but he gave up as his own pain became unbearable. He gathered up his things and left the classroom a few moments in front of the police, got into his car and drove off to the Back Door Inn.

"Can't ya take a joke?" Mike whispered hoarsely, and then fell silent. The Back Door Inn was an innocuous lunch bar during the day, with old lady waitresses and alcoholics. Desmond greeted them as brethren and began to drink that day and hasn't quit since.

He told me as much himself. We traded stories one day in an empty boxcar of the Erie-Lackawanna Railroad during the New Depression, when everyone rode the trains, everyone drank, all of us said we were writers or should be written about, everyone had a story to tell. Had and will have as long as natural man survives.

I should say, first, that Desmond didn't believe my story either. But he let me share his bottle of muscatel on the condition that I listen quietly. When he was done with his tale I asked him if he'd introduce me to Mike. Des was still a young guy, but with that air of utter defeat. He was maybe fifty, though it's hard to tell with us. We don't care for mirrors much, and the juice has this strange aging effect. Miracle drug. Hurries us towards death. Leaves few lucid moments. Glad for my typewriter which I lug around with me everywhere, though it gets lonely now despite the tapping. Where was I. Yes. He produced Mike, Desmond did. Held him in his hand and yes, I could see that Mike must have been a grand strapping monster of a pecker in his former glory. But he just lay there, panting, like a beaten, wet dog, and I thought I heard a small whisper, but I might have been mistaken.

"Glad to meet you Mike. I feel as if I already know you."

"Come on Mikey," Desmond said. "Say hello to the gentleman. Ah, it's no use. He isn't very talkative any more. He's pretty despondent since he hasn't been able to stand up and salute. Yes, that's what he used to do. He'd stand up straight as a ramrod and greet me each morning with a snappy, 'Good mornin' to you, cap'n.' Hasn't done that in six years. It's the juice, you see. Well, of course you do."

We sat there with idiot bleakness on our faces, alternately pondering the extreme absurdities of a life that beat one down and then calculating when would be the soonest possible moment to reach for the bottle of muscy and take another deep swig without being too impolite. Out of this alcoholic haze, Desmond asked me suddenly, "What's your story, m'fren?"

"Well," I began with a sigh, clutching the bottle to my chest dramatically, hoping he would think it merely another sincere motion of the arm. "I didn't know what made me come to my typewriter that night. Perhaps it was the heat. The night was muggy and the two bodies in my bed were heat generators . . ." On and on I went, telling him about the story I had been writing, the story about this guy that has a talking penis, the discovery of Minette in my pyjamas. It was only then, I swear, that I noticed the strange coicidence, the confluence, the symmetry between the two small intelligent beings, Mike and Minette, and the disturbing accident of time and space that let Desmond and I share the same train on the same night, share stories as well. But my memory is so foggy. Did I write their story? How have I come to be a character in my own story and Desmond a character in my life? And who is writing this story, or are you just taking notes, you the one drinking my bottle of muscatel? And where is Minette? I seem to have misplaced her. Oh yes. That has always been my fear. That one day I would drink too much and roll over on her or crush her underfoot. No, I can't seem to find her anywhere in here, or did I really lose her long ago? No, she's not in this almost empty boxcar of the Erie-Lackawanna New Depression prose train, hurtling through the day, no . . . the night. It's too damned dark in here, with the sun going down day after day in a splash of bloody red on the cornfields. Minette and Mike? Ah. I remember now. She left me, though I could have killed her, squashed her between thumb and forefinger. Yes, she left me that same night with everything that had come to pass. Or perhaps I lied. Maybe she had never been. No little voice, no French accent, no perfect body, no divorce, no exurban home, miniature furniture. My litte Minette? You must be mistaken. She was nothing more than a morning muse. A predawn mix-up. A passing inspiration, she was mother to Mike, antemeridian messenger of a disappointed marriage, a marred mind . . . But then, if all that is true, why am I riding this train?

THE WORD ARTIST

"Quidquid predicis esto brevis."
—A Roman aphorism
"When you're on the brink, don't talk so much."
—The Word Artist's Father

The word artist did not originally intend to become a word artist. He was schooled carefully for a clerical profession from a very early age. Or, perhaps, it was the medical profession, or even the Bar. That is no longer exactly important. Indeed, the word artist has already forgotten most of the precise information about his past. His memory, even of his parents, is faulty. However, he is rather fond of quoting his father: "As my father used to say, 'Quid quid *precipice*, esto brevis. When you preach, don't talk too much.'" Then he laughs because of the obvious mistake his father had made, and people laugh along with him because although they are afraid to offend the memory of his father, yes they are more afraid of offending him.

The word artist does know that: "Well, there was a brief period of rebellion . . ."

Of course, it doesn't really matter if he is telling the truth or not. If he fabricated a little, or fantastically, he would claim he was revelling in his "delight in words." And who among us could fault him for that? This was early in his career. The word artist was still a popular figure in the small riverbank cafes. He affected a studied pose at the tables during this, his youthful period. Debating with the painters and poets and scribblers, he would denounce writing as "a subversion of the Pure Form." He called the theater "an unconscionable and lewd spectacle," working himself up until in a huff he would gather up his scarf and gloves and down the wine with defiance at some imagined slight before strutting away.

His performances occurred informally at first, in the shopfronts leased for him by a local newpaper and in the cafes. One day, he finally announced to our little circle that he was done with these amateurish productions, done with the informal debate, done with the idle conversation which compromised him. Again, he left in a huff. The next day he reappeared talking and debating all the old topics as before over a glass of bordeaux. Little Charles made the grave mistake of questioning him, though I dare say, we were all a bit confused.

"Well, I'm glad you've repented of your outrageous resolution," Charles exclaimed. "Imagine not wanting to *speak* to us!" Of course, we stared embarrassedly at Le Petit's boldness and looked away over the river as the word artist turned livid with rage.

"Speak to you! I am amazed that you could confuse this, this . . .*chatter* with my art!"

After that he returned seldom to us, and when he did, would sit silently in glum judgment, nodding assent with his eyes or motioning slightly with a gloved hand. Meanwhile, the local theaters were tearing down the large cinema screens for Friday and Saturday nights and erecting podiums in their place. The audiences would crowd in to stare up for hours at the thin young man in an impresario's tuxedo, as the time fairly flew, carried on the wings of his word magic. Interviews with him appeared, first in the daily city papers and then in the glossy magazines. Eager poets would rush to the newsstands, tearing out columns of fine print and pasting them on the walls of his old haunts or near their bedroom windows, those poets tired of writing.

Then came the invitations from universities and the patrons of the arts. High above the sordid city the artist entered a plush apartment, invariably late, and would be ushered into a roomful of the city's elite. The hostess would fawn over his coat, the mayor and his wife would bow graciously. Everyone would nod at his "Good evening," appreciating the gratuitous impromptu performance of his art. Once, an actor applauded raffishly, but then he apologized for his cynical gesture. "Sorry, old man. Just a joke, right?" He offered him a conciliatory drink.

With an uncharacteristic composure the word artist accepted his apologies, but later in the evening he could not resist that little mean impulse in him and said, "It is often said that actors are simps, oafs, louts, dolts, gawks, fools, drivellers, madmen, puerile, vacant, vacuous babblers, obscene and loafing ruffians. However, I wouldn't believe a *word* of it." The company laughed deliriously, complimented him on his rare and excellent wit, and nodded at each other to demonstrate their rare and excellent wit. Meanwhile, the rash—yes, I think it was an actor—slunk down to his auto and drove away cursing.

At the university he was invited to lecture. As he launched into an explanation of word art, literature students took notes eagerly, scribbled furiously, as the rest gazed (particularly the co-eds). Later, he entertained questions from the students. Once, or so the local newspaper reported, a brawl erupted in the auditorium when a sophomore (from the state school, it must be admitted) asked the artist how the distinction could possibly be made between his lecture and a performance.

"In other words, sir, what exactly is it that you do?"

The word artist stalked off stage.

The other students battered the dunce with paper airplanes and howls of execration. The boy yelled out some obscenity to his peers and he called the artist a "Charlatan!" even as he was dragged away by the entire senior class in comparative literature.

Known only to his intimates, the word artist had been in analysis for several years. His confessions would shock us, yet when pressed further, he would deny and deny. Finally, though, he blurted out to us that he was lonely.

"I don't know how to describe the feeling."

We looked around at each other, trying to gauge how to react to this remarkable statement, this admission of his insufficiency with the language.

"Everyone calls it 'loneliness,'" he went on, "but that has an impure taste on the tongue. I can draw no correspondences between the three syllables and that ineffable emptiness signified by the word. Yet," he sighs, "I am resigned to calling it such. Loneliness." We comforted him and asked him to please not hide behind his art. We are your friends, we told him. You can say to us what is really wrong, we said. He paused and cleared his throat, urged on to even more embarrassing revelations.

"And you must wonder why I am not always surrounded with terribly beautiful girls." Little Charles suppressed a snicker. The word artist was a notorious homosexual. "Why, he is always at those terribly chic parties, you say. And there is a certain envy in you, ah yes, don't deny it my friends. But, if only you knew. It is all vacant. Do not envy me. Pity me, rather and think of the irony. For there I could be with S. or charming K.—lascivious, ravishing—and instead of using all the right words—and yes, I know there are right words, for I have rehearsed them many times in my head and before the mirror—I find nothing but lewd puns are swimming in my head, or worse, *overwhelming visual images*." He shuddered but recollected himself. He stood in the middle of the floor and raised his finger at the heavens.

"Gentlemen, we can create art, but we cannot conquer it

unless we have conquered ourselves."

Solemnly, we shook our heads at our friend. We did not know how to help him and hoped his analyst had answers.

"No," he sighed again, "my analyst cannot help. He commands me to free associate, and more and more often I find that I have launched into one of my performances, my Pastoral Elegy, say. And once I start, I am helpless; I am compelled to see the thing through. In fact, I have often wished to record my couch monologues."

Again we nodded, this time in dismay at the trap the word artist had fashioned for himself.

It was not long after this incident that the word artist began a series of purges in his art. Already, you see, imitators had made bilge of the word artist's flow; graduate students wrote doctoral dissertations (usually entitled, "Word Art: The Birth of a New Form" or, "The Works of the Word Artist: Semantic Technology or Verbal Abuse?"); comedians burlesqued his histrionics; and television parodied his style, using only slightly reworked material.

The most memorable evening of the word artist's too-brief career was the first performance of this New Syntactical Period. The artist strode on stage, his usal tuxedo gone, replaced by black pants and a black turtleneck shirt. The house lights were cut and a spot appeared on him. On a signal, an older gentleman appeared and tied a single black ribbon around the word artist's wrists, behind his back. The attendant bowed and exited, leaving a moment when the artist and the crowd were alone with each other in silence. Grimly, and in a steady, familiar voice, he began to recite a string of words unbroken by punctuation, modulation, or gesture. The audience strained forward to capture the sense of his words but soon found themselves transported by the ineluctable sound of his slowly pronounced composition. Unconscious murmurs of pleasure rose to his performance. He gulped air, expanded his thin chest so he could sound out more words before he had to breathe again. He went on, impossibly on, for three hours, the potency of his words sending even the most shocked bourgeois into rapturous, reverent attention.*

At the finale the audience gave a thiry-minute ovation; women swooned, hands were chafed raw, lungs were scratched silent. The artist was persuaded to take an encore, and a tired but grateful crowd again sat, hushed.

The artist took a deep breath and uttered loudly, again in an absolute monotone, "THANK YOU." Wild cheers and foot stomping ensued for another five minutes until he left the stage and finally, the lights came up.

Urged on by this success he announced his plan to eliminate capital letters and the words "something," "right," and "obfuscate," which, he added, he thought were the most offensive in the language.

Meanwhile, he never appeared socially, refused lecture invitations, and sent a neatly-worded letter to the President begging his On High's pardon for his failure to attend the annual Artist's Ball at the Presidential Palace. Even his closest friends were turned away at the door to his flat by an unctuous Korean valet.

When I finally did get to see him he was thinner than before, prematurely grey, his face furrowed by lines of age and lorn. The strain of speaking in a monotone all these years had taken its toll. One could see the inner dismay at his yearnings, yearnings peculiar to a word artist. As he greeted me in his apartment he began a strange confession. This, too, he uttered in an absolute monotone.

ah my dear friend how sometimes i wish though you
must not reveal this how i wish for my days of carefree
youth days of commas and periods an occasional con-
traction perhaps would give such enormous satisfaction
my dreams my dreams are possessed by mad alien
languages guttural and loathsome sounds lunge at me in

*This text of this first performance has been widely anthologized, Cf. Plaisted, *Word Art Omnibus,* vol. I, pp. 3–109—Editor's note.

my darkness chaos confronts my every night and dread
my every day spent in composing what the nights have
undeciphered but what else is left me an unrhetorical
query only words is the answer only words emblazoned
on every true artists soul

His eye flickered with a kind of fear but was extinguished
by that pleading wet look that he wore now. Even in public it
could be distinguished, and the elite in the orchestra seats
noted that forlorn gaze as he walked on stage.

At the same time, his most moving and ingenious pieces
were composed. His comical piece on "Wedded Words" is
still the most popular. He believed that certain words were
wedded to each other, often unhappily:

carried away
prematurely grey
ill bred
pouting lips
repressed hostility
unrequited love
substantial contribution
physical pleasure

His most beautiful short pieces he called "Meditations,"
enchanting short odes contemplating the most sublime words
in the language. His oft repeated "Meditation on Deracinate"
is still popular.

deracinate	deracinate	deracinate
deracinate	deracinate	deracinate
deracinate	deracinate	deracinate

* * *

One year on the Coast I met the word artist accidentally,
in a seedy bar of a dilapidated resort town. My fortunes had
suffered. He was hiding behind sunglasses, but the unmistak-
ably thin brow and white scarf, now sullied, caught my
attention. At first I couldn't be quite sure, but I called out his
name once, softly, and then once again, more loudly. He

jerked around, his body tense, and almost fell off the stool upon which he was perched.

In the intervening years his popularity had plunged. It wasn't obvious whether the crowds had lost interest as his performances became shorter and shorter, more and more abstract, or whether he had simply refused publicity, seeking solitude to develop a more perfect diction. The word artist had indeed turned people away, purposefully or not. He never repeated a composition. Those who came expecting old favorites were soon disappointed. The acerbity of his style became brutal, and the compositions were confused jumbles of words, abstracted chains of syllables with no context or apparent reason. His voice jarred the bourgeoisie who had come to hear a mellifluent baritone; his unpredictability thrilled the students but also discouraged them: they had to develop theses on his work, and he cut them adrift from logic.

I greeted him warmly, trying to hide my surprise at his condition and my own embarrassment. He wore a shabby mockery of his former finery and spoke with a slur from the drink before him. We had had a falling out half a decade earlier, but all that was forgotten in the gloom. When he saw I was resolved to speak to him, he motioned away a queen (or a whore, it was difficult to distinguish in the dark) from his side.

vacationing here   he stated.   abhor other countries cant speak their languages

"Have you been performing?" I asked him.

no   he snorted, controlling it with an even worse cough that racked his body in a violent spasm.   finished   he added,   they dont understand

"Would you be insulted if I told you I've quite lost track of your stuff, old man? As you see, I haven't quite been riding the top of the Western world."

He motioned his arm heavily as though dismissing the thought of reciprocity. I had the impulse to ask him so many things as he gulped at his drink, but he enveloped himself in a sheath of silence. Word artists must also use silence, and he had been a master. Then, as if returning from some voyage

behind his cloak of thought, he began to talk, his words
jabbing out in pointed, mechanical syllables.

> when it first began it was only half serious how could it
> have been otherwise word art (ha) mere talking its the
> easiest thing in the world it was the only thing i knew or
> know how to do and somewhere i have forgotten how to
> be only half serious when i was younger i deluded myself
> i thought they believe in me then i had a vision that if i
> pursued the art long enough i could distill it refine it until
> THE WORD would be revealed to me it was a private
> vision that i dreamed in public places and was duly paid
> for THE WORD possessed me but never manifested
> itself in desperation i was driven to turn everyone away
> to abolish my own being to be able to hear to speak to
> give THE WORD to those who were all along never able
> to understand

His violent cough interrupted him. It sounded too uncomfor-
tably like consumption. When he resumed, his voice had
diminished to a mere whisper:

> how dare anyone take me seriously especially myself
> even you my old friend have heard now my last piece its
> title is self reflection and could not laugh though yes
> sometimes it feels as though i am living THE WORD
> and it will appear across my burnt years a searing
> obvious . . . but i do not understand i cannot read the
> signs

We sat in silence. He ordered another drink but I insisted
on paying, though I could ill afford it. After some moments it
was time for me to go, to meet my midnight appointment.

"Forgive me. We must write."

He just shook his head without turning to see me go,
drinking his scotch and hiding behind his sunglasses as I
slipped out into the humid night.

* * *

It was not long afterwards that I received a letter from an
old colleague of mine at the University. It described the word

artist's last performance. The letter told how he announced that he "finally understood" and would give a public performance. A mystified but devoted group of people emerged from the underground and assembled in the auditorium that the word artist had sponsored for himself: wild-eyed students, sceptical journalists, a few of the Old School, an occasional middle-aged couple fondly remembering the word artist of a more youthful, less confusing decade. In a program handed out (enclosed in the letter) was the following statement from the artist:

> to my friends and devotees i want to thank you for attending this my final perfomance the title of which is meaning

I quote my friend's letter:

"The small audience hushed; and electricity that almost captured the brilliance of former years pervaded the stage, as the single spotlight came up and the houselights were doused. Then, this tragic figure, this non-presence, our dear friend, the word artist. Ah, Frank, how it would have grieved you to see him! His rent clothes, his body diminished by half. It seemed he would need help to mount the very stool from which he was going to read. He cleared his throat with an awful wet gurgle that sounded through the hall like a death rattle."

My friend, as you can see from this letter, is a former novelist, but now only teaches at M_____ University.

"With the eyes of a prophet of old and an accusing stare that gleamed out into the darkness with an inner light he shook his head sadly, once and began a low, mechanical laugh.

ha

But the sound mounted in his throat, his terrible grim gurgle of a chuckle mounting, becoming a frantic bellowing laughter, a demonic, hysterical scream of mad glee, 'HA! HA!' resounded through the theater, 'HA! HA! HA!,' and then, silence. A terrifying silence. As suddenly as they had burnt, his eyes were out, closed, though his mouth remained agape, frozen wordlessly in a contorted scream, a wild, silent plea. The word artist returned to the eaves of the stage, and for all that we could tell, out into the night. For, after the group that had come recovered from their amazement, some of us ran backstage hoping to see him, asking him to explain. But he was gone. Only a deaf mute janitor sweeping up behind the stage greeted me with an ignorant and mocking smile."

And here my friend goes on to describe the weather at Lake Como and the preparations for his last daughter's wedding.

IMPERIAL PLACE

At last it is noon, and the incessant threatening noise has subsided. We are all gathered here, the remnants and the refugees: the old blind woman, the crippled boy, the mother and her suckling infant, myself. Ragged and distraught, I have no memory. The present seems to expand, the past is a series of discontinuous horrors.

I've lied already. See how I've been corrupted! I remember all too well my predicament. I know the past as only the criminal knows, though I don't know what crimes I've committed or why what has happened has happened. Listen. The gunshots are starting. Outside. Inside this chamber we fight incessantly—the five of us—over the few coins we have left, though God knows it's useless. At dusk the old woman falls asleep, and I steal over to her side unnoticed by the others. I rob her cache—a few silvery or copper coins—and stuff them in my shirt. Then, at night, the young mother comes to me to make love, moaning and whispering in her strange tongue.

"Ansala mindhashu, shhh, menami minshani, ooooh, shevi-shevi."

While I am at the peak of my excitement, she slips her hand into my discarded shirt where she has seen me hide my prize and takes it for herself, all the while deceiving me by greedy contortions of love (or lovely contortions of greed) to make the shirt accessible. When it is over, she cries (in remorse?). I fall asleep.

Then, a few hours before dawn, amid the gunfire and screams, at a few hours before dawn, when the chaos is at its peak, the crippled boy (he has no legs) crawls on his over-long arms to the woman and grasps her neck. His torso is powerful; he makes her gurgle assent to his demand for money. The baby cries and clutches with his little fist clenching and unclenching the dried-up breast of his mother. At dawn I awake and beat the boy into submission. I kick him until the few coins slip out of his hands and gather them up. The old woman, however, is supernaturally quick. Surreptitiously, with the invisibility of the blind, she hides them in her rags, returns to her corner and sniffs in minor triumph, preparing me for the beginning of a new cycle.

This has been going on for many many days. Time, our only hope, is vanquished. Days are sullied by arid dreams.

I.

I was too diffident to be a good ambassador. They sent me from assignment to assignment, and I drank my way out of every one. Finally, though afraid to be quite rid of me because of my father's influence, they ran out of continents. So they sent me to that place. When I first arrived there that time it was a time unlike any other. The people were dangerous and mad, struck by an ineffable madness; the people were swept out of their homes, their miserable hovels, into the streets, where they looked for . . . They were small and dark, their primal faces and darkling smiles sent quivers down my spine the first time I stepped off the plane. In my own country, the few of this race that I met were shy and polite. But then in the airport, I stood above them like a lighthouse threatened by a dark broiling sea. Their emissary met me. He smiled, but he did not shake my hand. Instead, he gripped my arm at the elbow and guided me towards a waiting car. In a moment of panic I noticed that men waited inside the dark, behind the tinted windows, and I was about to rebel, to turn back and board the next plane home. The emissary's grip was firm. The door opened and I got inside.

I checked into the hotel, the biggest hotel of their country. It draped the flags of many nations, but this somnolent country understood nothing of politics or their own unfortunate future. They strove here in the city to forget the jungle past which lurked just a few kilometers from its heart: always ominous, always threatening to absorb them in its entropic engulfment, to siphon off the energy from human works. The structure of the city was a grand sieve; it leaked human effort back into the natural universe.

I never got to see the famous ruins that their ancestors had built. Somehow, when I looked into their eyes I could sense the uncreation of jungle life. Ragged urchins carried those ruins in their dull little bodies and their dingy eyes. I no longer wanted to see the giant stone temples for fearsome gods who ate babies and virgins in burning oil . . . potent incantations muttered by an ancient civilization . . . monster children . . . carnivorous birds . . . gold phalluses . . . rivulets of blood down stone steps . . .

II

"Yes, Lord, we have your reservations, Lord. Room 244, Lord. We hope the Sir will enjoy his stay. There is much the Man would like to see, perhaps in our country." The clerk exchanged significant looks with my escort. "It is small, but it is beautiful, and we are proud of this city. No? With its new stadium for the football and the water fountains in the plazas. Yes, I'm sure the Lord will enjoy his stay."

"Thank you very much. Oh, by the way . . . is it always this hot?" I had already stained my white suit, the dark pools of moisture steaming under my arms. I needed a drink.

"Oh yes. This is the dry season, Lord . . . heh, heh, the

dry season is just beginning, Sir, but in July, it will rain, and then it rains for six months. So you see, Lord, it is as we say here: 'If it is not the lizard, it is the fish.'"

III

As I was flying over the jungle for the first time (and certainly for the last, now that the airports are destroyed and the radios are silent) I could see the brown and scorched rim around the city. I could sense the lassitude of stange birds that were singing indifferently in the treetops.

In the hotel room I collapsed on the bed and took a bottle of whiskey that had been sent up, imported from my own country. The bottle stood in the silver cooler, and I was thrilled, savoring the moment, almost hesitant to open it, to break the virgin seal; it was a religious moment. A sizable puddle of water had already formed, the ice cubes losing their battle against hostile heat.

When my race first encroached here a century ago (do I sound cynical?) these people had already forgotten the science of their ancestors who had plotted the universe so they could be more emphatically chained to their own existence: the scrawlings on overgrown walls were ciphers, meaningless. They thought we were gods, deliverers, sent from the white sun. In exchange for their worship we gave them syphilis; their labor was returned with confoundment, their gold, with death. That is why they called me *Ansa Cantu*, Demon from the Sun.

I walked the streets in the empty morning, wending through the narrow alleys and then lounging near the broad plaza, sipping wine in view of the fountain. I meandered along with the bicycles and cars, followed by the inevitable band of urchins crying for bread or a token coin, their arms outstretched in supplication to the Demon from the Sun, as though I could forgive them as well as feed them.

"Ansa Cantu, please Ansa Cantu, munnah (money) Ansa Cantu." They made wild, horrible gestures, stuffing their fingers into their faces and squeezing their bloated bellies.

"Please Ansa Cantu."

IV

In the University, for a while, I wanted to be a poet. But I never succeeded; I was too unsure and would never be able to stand the sight of someone reading my poems nor tolerate the sounds of someone else's voice missing the obvious stops, inflecting in the wrong places. My poems seemed treacly-blooded and self-conscious when I saw them through others' eyes. The anticipation of that siphoning off of meaning and significance prevented me from writing at all. Grand poetry was conceived in my head. Once (only once) I wrote four significant lines, lines that I had felt seared across my brain in the kind of burning dreams that only whores or students have, a slogan for my life. I awoke sweating and crying and wrote in mute appreciation (horror) the fate of the world:

wretched and wild and driven to violence
THE PEOPLE REMAINING become witness at
last to a TEMPEST this day.
ON THIS LAST DAY IT THUNDERS ON THE EARTH.

V

After a week I could not venture out of my hotel without becoming completely overwhelmed. The heat, the foreign faces, the alien air breathed through alien lungs—seemingly alive with virulence—would exhaust and terrify me in an hour. Once, I rushed into my room and pulled the curtain shut as though to blot out the city and sun. I drank my whiskey until the reminiscences of a boyhood swallowed my fear. I remembered wheatfields and wild horses, feeding the chickens. But these are someone else's memories, not mine. No, they certainly didn't seem like mine. Didn't I grow up in Brooklyn? It wasn't my boyhood I was remembering, or was it?

In my drunken impotence, I remembered those lines which had become less strange to me now, years later. Rebelling against the void in the eyes of these people, a vacuum I could not resist but which repulsed me with the strength of a race, I sat on the plush carpet and scrawled my lines on the wall with a slimy, indelible ink. In a rage, I carelessly slopped the message on the walls of the most beautiful hotel in the only city of this, The Serpent's Province.

VI

In the jungles, the children go to sleep with a small pot or bowl. They put pieces of dried fruit or sugar in them, so as they sleep their souls will be tempted by the treat and not escape; the souls will gorge themselves and fall asleep also, merging with the candy. In the morning, in that childish interim consciousness between wakefulness and sleep, they eat their souls and say a prayer of thanks.

There in the city the horde of nameless wild children are always hungry, wretched. They sleep among rusty tin cans and twisted chromium junked from the few cars. They sleep uneasily, have lost their souls long ago, suffer from scurvy.

VII

War had broken out, beyond the jungles. Day by day the men disappeared and were carted off in open boxcars on the railroad to substitute their urban anonymity for a uniform and mechanical death. Motion ceased. Little shops and stands closed. The trollies stopped running. The women who could not feed their children sent them away or drowned them mercifully. The listless heat of the city was usurped by whisperings, insidious scurryings, and the flitting shadows of ghosts and children seeking them. Hungry urchins filled the stooping doorways and gnawed inexorably at the city's carcass. Shops boarded up were burst open, stands were overturned.

In the mornings after impossibly hot nights, the streets would be littered with cans of food, dead bodies, both half-eaten and already diseased by flies that hovered everywhere in dizzy flight.

On the radio, sanguine speeches could be heard: uncontrolled voices of their leaders would break in frenzy, swollen with their lying. Little generalissimos would stand five feet tall in perfect white uniforms, in the squares, urging their people to bravery. Old withered men chewed gum and nodded off to sleep/death in the heat.

VIII

I was nearly alone in the hotel. A few old clerks and young maids (they whored at night, would slip into my room after winking at me in the hall; I would wait, sweating, naked, alone, for the scratch of a key in the door . . . with the turning of the knob my prick would rise . . . thirteen-year-old girls squirmed on me, briefly, robbed me when I slept) could be heard occasionally, and then, never. I owned nothing. I owed everything. I was robbed continuously until it was a joke, and I would leave small offerings outside my door (a wristwatch, a shoe, an empty bottle, a dirty sock—these people had lost their sense of value). The alcoholic days and vomitous nights ran together in a sleepless blur. My light brown beard began to grow. The liquor was gone, so I drank their stinking sweet wine out of ceramic jugs. I never ventured out.

Then the shooting started. At night. The distant and not-so-distant crackings of their toylike rifles punctuated my hours. When they finally came so close that I could see them running across the square holding their toys, I finally understood that they were children, and that the hours strung together in my life were an enormous hoax, the necklace toy of a crazy *enfant terrible*, the spoiled infant god of the jungle.

The smells of puke and piss were everywhere in my room; flesh and bones burnt and cracked outside. I never ate or changed my clothes. Hallucinations—storms of thought—blew through my head. The jungle, war, children, flies were consuming and consumed there. I opened my window only once. It was twilight, before sunup or after sundown I can't remember I can't be sure but I saw ten or twelve children dancing no surrounding a young woman a girl really holding her with the strength of animals preventing her from crying out no she was screaming as they ripped her clothes from her body and beat her her small taut breasts quivered and bled her eyes bulged as they moved I could almost see no I could see her bloated bellyhungerpregnancyfat no I could see her pregnant belly yes she was pregnant they were clutching at her tits shoving each other away so they they could suckle as she lay writhing and then unconscious until they left as if by signal scurrying away left her with a gratuitous kick each biting the hand kicking the tit that fed them. I stood at the window trembling, cowardly, transfixed. A moment later one of the older children returned and calmly stuffed the thin barrel of his rifle into her shoved the rifle into the socket of her poked the rod into her eye and pulled the trigger a little geyser of blood splurting from the hole. The body quivered a second. He ran back into the shadows. I turned away and rushed into the water closet to puke.

IX

The city burnt as well. One night, the smell of sacrifice was strong as flames shot high into the night illuminating the skirts of the sky, talking at the buildings. Already, blistering waves of heat splashed over my street, forcing me out of my room into the hallway. I finally had to leave the Grand Hotel, stripped, cut adrift from all that was familiar. I watched as the proud signs of engraved marble sootied and cracked and fell into the pavement. I ran into the alleys, losing myself in secret turmoils.

But I was pursued. The children were everywhere, whooping and slavering, running in naked packs. They chased me through the streets and paths so narrow that I could touch the opposite walls with my outstretched arms. I was a harried Goliath as they exploded shots into my legs and arms. Demon girls. Shots into my gut did not penetrate very far, but evey pull of the skin taut, every motion, was hell. The wounds festered quickly. Little infectious buds appeared as the small birdshot crawled deeper, seeking the roots of pain. Other adults were pursued and felled like great beasts by the little hunters. In every doorway I was sought out and aimlessly pursued.

I wanted only to die, to surrender.

BUT THEN THE FEARS WERE SLOUGHED OFF MY SOUL, and I realized that this—the festering wounds and the raging maelstrom of heat and history—was the true order of things. Revenge come into its own, everything was in its place.

Yes, perhaps. I'm really lying again. Somebody else's soul I'm talking about. *I* still huddled in the crevices or feigned death. Sometimes, I saw through closed eyes the hunter children, the hunger children, running on all fours, their rags hanging loosely over their backs, draping over their ribs. The jungle had come, and we, the children, the dogs, the flies and I, were all aimless refugees trapped by Nature's will. But I . . . was only a mindless rodent . . . no, a grub, a worm. I burrowed into the humid, rotting earth and fed on the dirt and wastes of a race. I feed even now and excrete little perfect nitrogenous crystals.

My legs were crippled from the sores out of which a nameless ooze flowed. Swarms of flies settled on me in the daytime. Somehow, I had crawled into the broad plaza through upended cars and inert newspapers announcing VICTORY! The shooting ceased at dawn as always, and the children returned to their holes to whisperchantscream their nightmares, their vindications in high voices.

I lay near the impotent fountain on a heap of dead bodies and broken, fallen stone cherubim, eternally pouting, broken-winged or decapitated. I played with the flies. I allowed them to eat me for a few moments and then shooed them away with the slightest of gestures. Then, I hummed to myself, a time later, quietly. And then, I made a phone call to an old high school buddy. Then one to my ex-wife. She was fine, but said she couldn't talk right now, so I promised to call her later. I never did. I knew that my buddy and she were cheating on me. My parents said they were ashamed of me. They clucked their tongues, and mother pointed at my soiled pants.

"You've made yourself caca," she said. "Why didn't you change your clothes?" She clucked her tongue again. My father removed his spectacles, a secret signal I understood to mean he was

REGISTERING DISAPPROVAL.

The dead bodies around me sat up and confessed that they, too, had played with their flies, had feigned death, and caused their parents to be ashamed. The cherubim played rock and roll. The sun disappeared in a bloody mess at the end of the boulevard. I stumbled back into the surrounding streets—narrower and narrower—they choked me until I grew unsupportably big, painfully gigantic.

A sniper ran up to me a few yards away.

For a few seconds she just looked at me, eye-level with my belt. Her wide brown eyes, her smudged face, talked to me, asking me, telling me . . .

"Papa," they said.

"My child," I held out my arms to her, smiling, leaning my back against the door, sinking slowly on legs that melted.

"This is where I belong," I thought.

"My child," I said to her. With a warm and beautiful smile she just looked at me and giggled, putting her tiny brown hand to her face to hide her smile.

She held her needle-thin barrel to my belly and shot. It was the first shot of the evening, and I heard her giggle again as I crashed through the door.

X

When I awoke, I was here with my friends: the blind old woman, the cripple, the mother and her wasted infant. Perhaps I am dead, and this is some joke of a purgatory. That thought has occurred to me today. It is my interesting thought today. The pain in my gut, the big black one, never subsides, though.

It is dusk again. Time for me to rob grandma over there. Perhaps she is ready for me. She must have noticed the pattern after all these . . . months? She never ceases her fervent mutterings to her strange god. Or maybe, this is her purgatory, too. What crimes has her flesh committed in all its withering years?

Me, I wait for the love moans of the mother, though she is a thief in the night, stealing my seminal hopes, my coins. But then, there is the triumph of beating the crippled boy and avenging my pitiful lover.

III

ROPE DANCES

AN EVENING IN HELL WITH SAMMY AND ANITA

There was the faint whirr of distant machinery and an authoritative click and then . . . silence. It was the oldest story in the world: he awoke and found he was somewhere he shouldn't be, wearing a monstrous unfamiliar body, an old consciousness trapped in a new form . . . almost as though he hadn't woken at all.

But this time someone had fouled up. His wife had come along. Though he couldn't see her in the gloom, the familiar tugging at the bottom of his stomach every time she would speak was there, yes, with the recurring acid hiss of delicate tissue consuming itself, the gaseous rumblings; all the symptoms were there, and twenty-seven years of habit told him, therefore, that his wife was there, too. After all, a man's body has its own logic.

But where was her voice? He was used to tuning her out, sure, but it was so quiet here. Oh! he thought, and reached to turn up his hearing aid. Still can't get used to this damned gewgaw, defective goddamned jap box they got stuck in there. On clear dry days he would pick up the AM radio. Waking in the morning after a night of uneasy dreams he would hear

I was in the right place,
But must have been the wrong time.

His stomach hissed again, this time with a weird foreign twang, and he found he could not reach at all, no, not even to the little tuner on his chest which adjusted the volume.

He couldn't reach because he had nothing to reach with.

Tug . . . tug . . . the rope pulled at his belly.

Damn dark, too. Couldn't feel his legs.

No arms, no legs.

Don't panic man. Car accident? No, last night I sat and plotted the murder of my wife.

Sammy had become a grey burnt-out lump of flesh.

A rope hangs in the distance still. It can't be approached too closely, and only dim shapeless forms can be made out at either end. A little fresh smoke still hung about them back then, but now it is rather clear . . . a terrible clarity reigns there . . . or perhaps, then, it was only moisture steaming off into space as the dessicating process began to end.

The rope between them, a gross insensitive affair, should have been only the thinnest of delicate threads, registering their every comment and sign. Instead, an old tie-line, a hauser, bound them to each other, and a bit of tarry odor mixed in with the after-burn stink to make that space around them so completely unpleasant.

Yet, no light, no heat nor the perceptible lack thereof.

The creatures, Sammy and Anita, seem confused. There is a certain something about them—the ineffable, say—a cosmic shrug of shoulders, an invisible suspension of the comic question mark over the two lumps that gives one the impression of confusion. Those two beings, there for the first time in their new forms, still struggled to retain the wisps of their former lives, which misted and occluded their belief in that moment. How could this have happened to them?

Anita thought that Sammy had tried to murder her and had botched it up. She didn't even trust him to do that without making a mess of it. She was suspicious of those long silences in the evenings, the furtive, fugitive resentments lurking through the nights. Though her body was surprised at this new sensation of death, she had long been expecting something like it. Sam's strangeness, the catatonic evenings at home, the deep hollows of his eyes and the bags beneath them that accumulated pendulous weights of secret intentions, all these could not hide his fierce mental activity. Anita knew he planned sedulously, continuously.

Perhaps he only half killed me on purpose, leaving me to smell this hellish brimstone and burnt-flesh stink wafting from my own corpse. Perhaps he meant only to wound me, torture me with the immense pain of skin burnt to the final degree.

When sure of just anybody's hate, you cringe and plot and spend your time forming useful defenses, hating in return. But, sure of the hate of your lifelong cell-mate, your fellow prisoner, you lay on your cot and fear, hunker down and stay afraid, watching every movement, creating phantom motives, feeling the sharp edges of small objects, the porousness of a potentially suffocating pillow as you press your face into it in a paranoiac's limbo. You begin to invent sly circumstances to test the strength of his hand against yours. You wonder how dangerous it is that he always wins the lucky part of the wishbone, and what it is he wishes for. Anita had read in *Cosmopolitan* that her womb could be exploded like a balloon if Sam blew a lungful of air into her vaginal cavity. That night, and every night after, she wore tight panties to bed. She also cancelled her subscription to and burnt the magazine. She lay awake nights, cautiously watching his insomniac watchfulness. She spent hours in the library reading about lethal and toxic substances: specifically, the tasteless, colorless, or odorless; she began to watch for the smell of almonds; she placed locks on the cutlery cabinet and discreetly carried little aerosol cans of mace.

She thought of the enormous knots of flesh she had found

dangling in the pants of one of Sam's junior research assistants and the tactile temptations, the secret suppers she had enjoyed in-between his younger thighs.

. . . . In that instant . . . . she knew, with a sinking mental vertigo, that something had really happened to her. Her thighs did not warm as they should have; her ass did not squirm and go taut against the bed; her cunt did not begin to heat and wet. With a sudden jerk, a spasm of uniform and total pain radiated from her gut outward across her body; it felt as though someone were trying to suck off her skin, to tear it in one piece from her body as she had seen it done to a rabbit once. From her breasts, her belly, her thighs, her head . . . in one jerk . . . her body a confused mass of painful parts.

Sammy had just returned from Tokyo. He had occupied Japan to clean up the debris of a strange war. He had already acquired a taste, a salivating taste like the taste of blood, a sweet taste and loin-thrilling taste for the dusky women foreign enough to charge him with a superior potency, a feverishly electric sensuality not allowed him with the paler races. The sense of nuclear taint now only heightened this deliciousness. These yellow ladies, nut-brown ladies, awoke the boiling blood of the semites in him, placing a thin umbilicus of hot spiritual flesh between him and his mediterranean ancestors.

Back in Brooklyn, he leaned against a lamppost on Troy Ave. catching the scent of slightly burnt skin floating against the muggy exhaust of machines and men on a day nearing night. When he felt a sudden flow of sex begin to talk against his own heartbeat, he lifted his eyes to the twilight sweet vision of Juanita, ripe rum fruit of Puerto Rico, passing him by but not wanting to, catching his eyes in the cups of her bra, the dark body sight making animal pressures on his brain. He asked her to his room.

"Jou wan' take me to ya room?"

"Yes."

"S'funny. Lesterday, man ast me same ting. I say, 'No.'
Today, I say jes." She laughed.

"Why is that, Juanita?"

"When jou smell me, see me, jou tink real *bad* tings."

Once in Brooklyn, a fire flared up in a small girl's room, a
fire from the cigarette she had left burning on her dresser. A
fallen-asleep-eight-year-old Puerto Rican girl. An eight-year
old, she shouldn't have been smoking, shouldn't have fallen
asleep, shouldn't have been caught in that fire, shouldn't have
been caught by the whip of burning drapery as she struggled to
open the window.

The material caught fire and flared up, burning her flesh
as she screamed. Her skin served as wax to the curtain's wick.
Then, years later, after Sammy had indeed taken her to his
room, after he had reoccupied Japan in her Latin body, with its
burnt memory, after that incredible orgiastic night, the sun
came up over the Eastern Parkway and shone its red reflection
into the room, and while she slept, he slowly lifted the sheet
from over the burnt and scarred half of her body which he had
felt—but she would not let him see—all that night before. In
the red light, he watched the unbelievable pits and taut
tissues, the bridges of skin which stretched between craters and
unexpected lumps, knots, twists that the tortured surface of
her body took. Her skin had become a map of disaster, and he
read his way along it for many hours in the speechless
morning, taking a silent arduous journey over the moonscape
of her belly and thighs. The landmark mountain of her right
breast was still charred, still smelt faintly of smoke, though she
anointed herself every day with too much cheap perfume.
That, then, is the dusky ancient smell she has, that, the vivid
scent of racial ruin . . . betrayal . . . sacrifice . . . so attractive
and so unspeakable when she passed me last night. And
that tit, that tit sat on the wasteland of her torso, now a symbol
for something new and awful in Sam's new and awful
condition. He, too, was a burnt-out tit in the center of a
nihilist's nightmare, tethered to some image of himself, some
mocking Other who might be his wife.

With this recognition, Sam gave an involuntary jerk, and Anita on the other end opened her mouth to scream, only to discover that she had no mouth.

The rope jabbed and jerked the other way, giving her the same relief a scream would, but making Sam want to scream in turn.

Just as Sam was about able to shake the feeling that his wife had indeed accompanied him here; just as Sam conjured the thought that perhaps he was only the subject of an excruciating experiment, perhaps in his own laboratory, strapped to biofeedback and monitoring devices, hundreds of micro-electrodes implanted in his brain, others buzzing and shocking his genitals into NUMBNESS . . . EXCITEMENT . . . NUMBNESS . . . ; just as Sam was beginning to tell himself fictions, science fictions, about frankensteins and forgetfulness, with flat-chested graduate assistants and efficient Chinese technicians surrounding him, yellow men taking careful notes on yellow pads, watching the slow drip drip of his bottled intravenous meal—Sam strapped down, monitored until he was minotaured, made monstrous by the neural apparatus; just about then was Sam reminded that the insipid repetition of painful jabs into his gut, the feeling of paralysis and hopelessness and vacuity could only be no worse than his marriage, a marriage which had undergone this grotesque transformation.

Sammy and Anita now vied against each other in a strange struggle, a titanic tug-of-war, a spasmodic minuet, an agonizing rope dance, a spastic dance in space. There, where nothing was familiar, and a sightless world made everything doubtful, lost everything to the human sense, where there were no birds, no walls, no rooms, no wood-lined paths, no midnight meetings, no deep armchairs, no bloody newspapers with messages scrawled in its columns, no outside and inside, no points of reference save the two bodies in space, no desire to refer, no summer smells, no queen of hearts, no electron spin spectroscopy, no intermediate nuclear particles and all that they imply: kinship systems of the Maori . . .

paper clips . . . collisions in the sea . . . Anglo-Catholicism . . .
no Mycenean victory of Partahullis sometime in the twelfth
century B.C. . . . no Bronx . . . no dirty laundry, skeletons in
the closet, meanings, symposiums and arguments, no murder
weapons, no bravery, no rubber hoses; yet here, in hell,
eveything so familiar to the two creatures had been tragically
incarnated.

So familiar were their lies and accusations (as familiar as a
wet dream turned bad, as familiar as the fading response to
pain of an amputated arm is to the amputee, the ghostly
motion in the air of its absence while it is already a
decomposing part, subsumed in soil, picked at by vultures,
grubs, flies, vermin brood, oxidized into the air, reduced to
nitrogenous waste, in short, become part of the finely tuned
but grossly insensitive affair we call the Natural Universe)—
THAT FAMILIAR, THAT PERTINENT, THAT INDIF-
FERENT—that there they hung like burnt nippleless tits, like
scarred chewed tongues wagging at each other in quick thrusts
along a rope in space.

Sammy studied his newspaper though he held it sideways. He had scribbled minute notes in the column in letters
smaller than newsprint. It would take a magnifying glass to
read what he had written:

MURDER YOUR WIFE. "HOW TO" INSTRUCTION
PACKET 17

Go into the kitchen. With a lot of clatter and casual noise search
for a long knife. At least a six-inch penetration will be needed
to assure the student that his efforts will bear fruit.

As you can see, Sammy was a man of great whimsy.

Remember that murder is a fair enterprise and has a
demanding code of honor all its own. Let her suspect. Leave
room for the ambiguity of your own motives. Sharpen your
knife on the noisy electric sharpener. Call out to her. She will
not respond. Turn up your hearing aid. Then yell: "Come
forward and meet your maker, *macha, macho,* monster, mister,
master, *maven* . . ."

A man of great whimsy, Sammy was also very fastidious. He

had been writing instruction packets in his newspapers for months now. A year ago he would draw his own cartoons in between "Andy Capp" and "Gasoline Alley" or "Pogo" and "Blondie." *First Frame*: Man sits in armchair with evil but pensive face, reading newpaper. *Second Frame:* Man in kitchen brandishes knife, the drawers are open, menacingly. *Third Frame:* Man sharpening knife. Balloon reads, "ANITA" *Fourth Frame:* and so on.

After the comics he would write news items, headliners:

KITCHEN KILLINGS

New York City, April 12—Police today have apprehended the suspect in a grisly murder of a Brooklyn woman today. The victim, her identity as yet undisclosed, was found in a puddle of her own blood the object of a vicious knife attack in the kitchen of her ranch-style home. When police responded to an anonymous call, the victim's husband was found on the scene, calmly eating a corned beef sandwich on rye with mayonnaise.

While Sammy wrote instructions to himself, Anita lay on her bed, her spreading thighs slightly raised, slightly parted, her head sunk deep in her pillow, her breasts large and globular and fat also spreading, quivering in two uninviting masses. Her hair could be seen as a slightly luminescent, lurid glow, hair so red that it seemed to say, "Yes" to every deep and warning "No," though now the body was bigger, more embracing, and the head beneath the hair so high in reefer, so lost in the tense reefer haze of the slightly paranoid. In one hand she held a fat joint; in the other, she played with a long fat length of red tubing, the kind of rubber hose she worked with in tenth grade chem lab, the kind of rubber hose she always conjured when thinking of Sammy's lab. She envisioned rows and tiers and a chaotic tangle of flexible lines jerking and twitching as unknown liquids coursed through its living body, tubes leading around and through each other to such a complex degree that they finally meant nothing. When sixteen, she was beaten by the same kind of rubber hose in the hands of a boy on the varsity wrestling team.

"Where did you get that hose?"

"From chem lab, where else? Now lay quiet and take yer fuckin' medicine."

"Don't leave any marks."

Wrestling Star would beat her in earnest, and the same look would come into her eyes as when other boys would ride her, ride her in long high loops that would take their thing against her thing and then down deep until her fever matched theirs.

How ironic to kill him with this. I wonder if I am strong enough.

She read in *Cosmopolitan* that rubber hoses are the tools most easily employed in strangulation. It was in a four-page spread on Domestic Squabbling with full color photos showing a subtle wristy technique that reminded her of a tennis backhand.

Through the muffling hootchie haze, in the reefer refraction she had thrown around her senses, she heard a grinding sound. It came to her slowly that the electric knife sharpener was being worked by Sammy. *He probably wants a corned beef sandwich.* Almost by reflex, she got up to help him. "You're not going to have Anita to kick around any more," she murmured. Her hand grasped the hose tightly, her knuckles white and numberd. A tautological beer commercial she didn't want to remember floated in her head.

In New York City, where there are more Puerto Ricans than in all of Puerto Rico, more people drink Rheingold beer than any other beer.

Sammy heard her footsteps. She had forgotten to take her bathrobe, and she noticed with off-color happiness that the linoleum was cold, the air was chilly after the warm bed. She wondered what she looked like and stopped in the long hallway to consider herself in the mirror. She was fat. Sammy heard her footsteps.

Frowsy bitch.

The rubber made a slithering hiss as she dragged it along the floor. In the kitchen, she stopped. Seeing her, Sammy gave a long, low moan of fulfillment and stood quietly watching her sway stupidly in the air, the hose strangely alive and intelligent at her side. Remembering something undone, he wanted to rush to the living room and see the paper's instructions. Instead, rooted, senses routed, he yelled, "ANITA!" though she was only five feet away. "ANITA!" he yelled, knowing she wouldn't respond. The tubing was doing a subtle wavy rope dance on the floor, undulating in time to the natural sway of her hips; still hissing, it seemed to slap its tail in anticipation. Sammy waved his knife in answer to the threat and began to circle her slowly.

Across the street, a neighbor absently walking his dog peered into the broad window of their house. Lit up at this strange hour, he could see the two of them dancing together in the kitchen. The little poodle squatted against the curb, letting out a small whimper of satisfaction as a shiver shook its bowels. The neighbor thought Sammy and Anita a lucky pair. He turned away guiltily, guilty of his own voyeurism, turning away as they embraced.

Sammy plunged the knife into her side as she wrapped the rubber tube around his neck and pulled, but the knife caught the tube first, fastening it into her body, tucking it between her ribs as she fell, pulling the tube taut, falling with all her weight, choking Sammy to death as she died, the rubber tube stretched now between the two corpses.

Sammy and Anita are still there in hell. Their flesh does not moulder. It is regenerated by the necessity of their tug-of-war. This paradox cannot be resolved; it is demonic. Frozen yet in their image of pain and hate, they are mobile enough to continue to inflict that pain on each other eternally.

Perhaps they will ultimately learn to speak to each other: learn a morse code of tugs along the rope that will approach language. Or, perhaps, their marriage by rope will become an art; they will find a small recompense in the aesthetic drama of their conflict.

More likely, they will grow tired of tugging; not tired of body, but of soul, and will finally find a pose most suitable, most symbolic, most subtle and there come to an eternal rest.

ROPE DANCE

1. The Game: A Description

To write of two tugging at each other, yelling at each other
across a coffee table in a country home, debating all the old
debates in a dance of words, a minuet: agonizing, deliberate,
repetitive. (In a minute: an agon, a deliverance, competitions
are all considered.) Sun shining or perhaps not shining. Hands
on knees. Four hands on four knees. Bodies against each
other but not touching. Squared away. Lips pucker, squirm,
close, clamp, glisten, rub, osculate, pout, vibrate, emit, suck.
Teeth dance behind the horizontal fleshy curtains. Noises are
gentle waves in the air. The two fall silent.

The eyes: two pair staring. Intertwining gazes clash in ambient
light, lock in frangible air. Extensions from eye to eye of
tangible lines. Spider threads. No, thinner than that. Thinner
still. Transparent. That would be ideal.

A line from eye to opposing eye.

Two tugging at each other across space along an imaginary
line in the ambient bluish light emitted by their eyes. That is

light so dim that only the most sensitive of creatures could actually see by it. Only the most sensitive of creatures would call it light at all, and not the gloom which it really is. Only sequestered and strange beings could exist in that darkness. Is there a lightbulb suspended midway over the thread of gazes which clash, melt into one another? No, we doubt that. There would be nothing to hold the lightbulb, nor anything to hold the holder, nor . . .

Tugging at each other across space along a far from ideal thread, a coarse rope actually. The two gazers are suspended in space and the rope is suspended by them. The suspension of all laws and of all forces real or imaginary: no gravity, etc., therefore, no walls, no birds outside the country home, no woodlined paths, no coffee table at all, no outside and inside, no points of reference, nothing to refer to, no desire to refer, no interlocking gazes, no summer smells, no postal system, no landscape, no words and all that they could imply: queens of hearts, electron spin spectroscopy, kinship systems of the Maori . . . paper clips . . . collisions in the night . . . Anglo-Catholicism . . . the Mycenaean victory of Partahullis sometime in the twelfth century B.C. . . . the Bronx . . . intermediary bozons, no meanings, no pen moving along a sheet of lined or lying paper, no author, no story being read to materialize among the synapses of the visual cortex.

Consider the sense of tension between the two bodies hanging, floating, or perhaps, absolutely still in space. It is the tension of a finite but definite animosity, an opposition, an antagonism; an irreconcilable, irrevocable ill-will given expression.

There is a rope, which in ripples—or better yet, oscillations— gives expression in its own language of signs, symbols, intensities, inflections to the intention of the two bodies toward each other. They don't make any sounds. No sound at all, for there is no atmosphere. No air nor lungs to breathe it, no ears, and it can be assumed, none of the other dependent organs. No heart to keep time, no regulation, no homeostasis, no stability in the pure and perfect stasis of these creatures who lack heart. The possibility of an event such as the heart beat is unthinkable to them.

The notion of time is also abolished.

Yet, the rope communicates to both information that is understood. Assume that they are able to communicate along the rope in the single dimension of the rope's linearity, the rope's narration. Assume sensitivities in the creatures: sensitivity to the rope's talk and an understanding of this language of tensions with its rhetoric and symbols, with a fluttering but continuous importance, with even a certain degree of tension which both understand to mean silence, understanding that even silence holds out meaning and that the evacuation of meaning makes meaninglessness impossible.

The animosity and opposition of these sensitives. Each holding out against the possibility of defeat by the other. The secret impenetrable core of understanding which believes that each is superior, stronger than the other, invincible. The conviction, the deep deep conviction that this superiority is ultimate, but that it cannot be communicated by the rope. The irritation that this insufficiency causes. The irritation as a cause of animosity. The animosity as a cause of the original conviction. The animosity as a perception which distorts the understanding of the rope's monologue, a monologue which is really a synthesis of the antagonists' dialogue.

The animosity as a response to the other's communications along the rope or to what each perceives the other's communications are, filtered through a haze of animosity.

The secret fear that each is alone and that the other does not exist. The same fear that the rope is tied to a tree or a stone or lightbulb. The same fear that the dialogue is really a monologue of the single lonely intelligence in space or a dialogue with the idiot rope, which would be the same thing. The way in which this secret fear alters. The fear that this secret fear is produced by the manipulations of the other. The fear that the rope does not exist or is hanging limply from the body as a cut umbilicus would.

These comparisons are obnoxious.

The fear that only the other exists.
The fear that only the rope exists.
The fear that . . .

There are periods, or at least, there is the notion that there are periods when the hostilities have subsided. These are periods of relative reconciliation. An almost light-hearted atmosphere prevails, despite their lack of heart. The rope is recognized as a shared bond, almost. There is, perhaps, a celebration of the rope and a deeper thankfulness that the rope is a line of connection in an otherwise lonely universe, an essential mooring of one to the other and not a barrier or a weapon equally shared equally resentfully. Jokes, or what would be called jokes, or what are their twiney equivalents of jokes—heavily barbed witticisms, in fact—are exchanged. Even the rope would be hard put to distinguish between periods of out-and-out hostility and these periods of relative reconciliation. Were they to stop and consult the rope and were the rope able to respond, then they would discover that it is all the same thing, the funniest jokes and the most vicious attacks. The only difference, it seems, is that the jokes have as their target the rope. Yes, during these periods of detente both agree to refer to the rope only, or so its seems. They unite in mockery of the rope as it becomes the butt of a thousand tired jokes.

Did you hear the one about the . . .

This is how the rope becomes the referee:

Each acknowledges the jokes to be referring to the rope. Each secretly fears and understands the joke to be directed towards itself, and harbors resentment, holds out secret animosity while waiting for the hostilities to resume so that the stored resentments can be vindicated.

The behavior of the rope and its implications. At times, from the complexity of the dialogue between the two, the rope appears to be assuming an intelligence of its own. If the rope were to be observed alone, ignoring for a moment the two creatures attached at either end, there is a definite surcharged meaning, a sur-meaning which would be made manifest and which it would be tempting to designate as "intelligent." (Tempting to whom?) In the language of this intelligent rope, the two appear to be mere terminals, anchors, static poles between which this wonderful sinuosity dances. If either of the beings were to stop and consider this, then they would be introduced to whole new realms of possibility. An entire realm of hitherto inconceivable meaning—monstrous or beneficent—would be realized. New views, shifting teleologies, bizarre cosmologies . . . Perhaps, if this idle fantasy is pursued, the rope would explain itself:

My dear friends . . .

Perhaps some resolution would be found, some ultimate reconciliation.

Since I have been cast in this uncomfortable role of referee, I thought it would be helpful if I pointed out . . .

Perhaps if each groped along the rope in order to seek out these hypothetical points of reference, of beneficence, the two would at some point, at some time, meet. The shock of recognition would overwhelm them. Ineffable sensations of . . . They would cower, repulsed with . . . Then, tentatively, they would seek each other out again. In time, an understanding, an accord would be reached. If this idle fantasy is pursued. (By whom?)

If each were to desert its post at the end of the rope, it would tumble impotently, limply, randomly, meaninglessly, irrevocably away. The secret fear that if each were to desert their posts at the end of the rope it would fall away, dangling uselessly out of reach.

Somehow, I remember the other. I know innately that we have touched somewhere before. I remember the other as pliant, handsome, pregnant with sensations for me that the dreaded rope never held out. I yearn secretly for this wishful . . . what? Memory? . . . to be true. Sometimes, I pretend that the rope is really the other, and I vibrate to it, caressing it with my organs, certain organs, trying to extract from it that memory of a single confrontation, a meeting, a coincidence in this sterile damned vacuum. Maybe we met more than once, clandestinely. Maybe we were lovers or best of friends, sprung from the same cause, intimate, inseparable, happily alone in a space undivided and unexplained and undefined by a single absurd thread which jabbers at me, yells at me, tugs at me even now with its absurd message, messages of hate.

Ah, but this is the rope trick again—a deceptive, crazy disappearing act—a message suggested by the other, sent by the other to lull, to deceive, to mesmerize me into that warm comfortable dream. Sometimes, in a vulnerable daze, I think to myself: if it has been, it certainly could be. But I must stop these vile habits of memory and caressings. Yet, I yearn miserably for the rope, symbol of the idyl, when I TRY TO STOP. It becomes the sole object of my desire. I want the rope, wrongly, I know, for all my own.

The way in which the rope possesses both by incarnating the desire in each to possess it. The secret secret way in which the rope causes them to possess each other by possessing them both.

The secret fear that victory would destroy the other. The fear that this victory would leave the victor alone. The fear that the rope is meaningless, and that though they vie and contend over it, submission to the other would be preferable to destruction of the other. The secret fear that each will yield to this fear.

Neither of the two remembers how this arrangement originated. Both are convinced that they did not create the situation. The way in which both create the situation. The fear that the other is creating the warring on purpose. The same fear, which is the fear that the other is a god for being able to create the situation. The belief that the other is a monster, imbued with terrible and dazzling powers of malevolence, shifting shapes, destructive rays . . .

The way in which the rope both excites desire and obstructs its fulfillment. The essentially alluring quality of the rope. Its beckoning by melodious monologues.

I can imagine dancing with the rope, alone with it, along with it, trying to match its beautiful curves, its strong snakey sinuosity, dancing a mincing minuet or a passionate polka or an erotic and sinuous ritual dance freed for one moment from the other. That is what I want.

Each recognizes that if the other is a god then it must be monstrous, deserving exorcism. Each recognizes that if the other is a monster, then it must be some kind of un-self-realizing god, utterly deserving victory.

The nature of the beings. Their grey and wrinkled exoderms. Their lack of any distinguishing features save a single dark hair up each smooth grey anus. The pliability of their grey skin. Their lack of vision for their lack of eyes. No appendages on them. The strange illusion that the rope merges with the skin, is woven out of flesh. The terrible greyness of the rope as it nears the body. The desires and fears which distort their self-images. The remarkable dream that has occurred to both of them that they are actually equipped with a plethora of appendages, buttons, holes, squeezing and squishing things, sprouts, extensions, false leads, wet caverns, obscene protruberances, hidden furs, prosthetic devices, vestigial organs, inner ropes that vibrate, paddles, wheels, shovels, viscous streams, gonads. The persistence of this disgusting dream. The way in which the dream acts on them to make them believe that they are monstrous.

<u>An example of an attack of one on the other:</u> First, assume the innate conviction in each that they are sane. The fear of insanity which causes this conviction to be clung to, desperately, in terror. The knowledge that to produce a conviction of this fear of insanity in the other would remove that fear from itself. The pretense of insanity by the aggressor. The sudden disruptions in the speech of the other, the disturbing but at first barely noticeable incomprehensibilities. The growing apprehension of these irregularities. The victim's initial attribution of the incomprehensibilities to a disruption in the other. The growth of the annoying but undeniable possibility that the growing perception of nonsense, mixed metaphors, oxymorons, paradoxes, self-contradictions, gibberish, pidgin phraseology, incomplete transmissions, inappropriate silences, unduly violent aggressions, undeserved compliments, inaudible but conspiratorial-sounding whisperings are all indications of an aberration, a rift in understanding for which only the victim itself is responsible. The incarnation of self-doubt. The confirmation of worst fears that this produces. The increasingly futile attempts by the victim to respond appropriately to these mixed messages. The existential flounderings. The alterations in behavior that these flailings produce: bizarre outbursts, duplicitous responses, continuous equivocations and evasions, long and guarded silences. The polite but firm suggestions by the victimizer. The mocking intimations. The increasing resort to fantasy and abstraction by the victim. The growing and remarkable potency of these fantasies.

The disturbing inability of the victimizer to abandon its pretense from long use. The distortion which the growing weirdness of the victim inspires in the victimizer. The concomitant self-doubt. The necessity for the instigator to educated itself in this new and crazy discourse of its opponent in order to maintain its manipulations, which are, after all, designed solely for the other. The alterations in behavior which this education enforces. The way in which the victimizer compulsively imitates the victim in order to manipulate it. The remarkable perfection of this imitation which prevents the victimizer from distinguishing itself from its victim. The growing comprehensibility of the victim's terror and madness. The strange reassurance this provides. The tendency to comply with the victim's fantasies.

The victim's gradual cure effected by the realization that it is no longer incomprehensible. The victim's growing conviction that its fear of insanity was only a fear.

The aggressor's increasing fear that its victim's madness was a fond wish confirming the victimizer's innermost fear. The ensuing madness.

2. They Play

I simply wake up. Though it cannot be said there is sleep here, there are certainly dreams.

Perhaps she was watching me, waiting for me, insidiously sending little flutters of subtle influence, guiding my dreams to their awful lies. And just why I think it is a she is no wonder, not after all this . . . this murkiness which occludes everything, confuses everything.

She is just far enough away from me not to know if she has an indentation which fits my protrusion, though I know she must, though my protrusion is imaginary.

And the dream,

Yes, I have known her before. I see the little shop, two steps down off the dirty sidewalk, a light tinkle of the bell, the opening door. It is a bookshop; I am a lousy student. Books, student, sidewalk, bell. Where and how do I know these things? Nouns I should have forgotten long ago.

To whom am I talking, thinking anyway? I know of woolen skirts and high-heeled shoes and auburn hair in a flip, tight sweaters over rounded breasts. Something out of a grade B movie . . . books lying haphazardly . . . an enfeebled father's bad system . . . Sneaking out as he falls asleep in his mis-buttoned cardigan, in his armchair, pipe pointing out of the ashtray towards the door. We slip out, she and I. Who is she?

Who is she? My prick thinks of hardening, my hands think of crawling under her sweater. What a joke! Now she floats out there on the tether, a grey burnt lump of flesh (a nippleless tit, or a bloodless, chewed lip, a discarded foreskin) reminding me of me, my mirror image. She makes me create her in my own image: a monster. Hating, fearful. Then, there are simple things, like the hair up my ass.

The rope burns terribly, its message searing into my flesh. The familiar odor of hamburger smokes off into space. She is saying, 'It is time now. We have had respite enough. You are not allowed to come crawling to me to be petted.'

   Fuck you, babe.

I tug on the rope, knowing it will distend her skin painfully.

But when things are nice; when we are caressing the rope simultaneously and it dances for us; when it is a little quieter around here; when I am almost alone, or can almost imagine that I am alone; when I think of a little bump here—a button, really—pushing out to the grey void, then to complete the universe, to satisfy unexpected cravings for, um . . . order, I allow a neat repository for it, a tiny hole, a small ripe crease, a tight-fitting fold, a comforting little cavern for it. I can clearly feel the bump grow towards its mate, a perambulatory peg undulating for its goal. All the other places exist on my rival. She is the only landscape here. Invariably, the socket inhabits her. These are small, wondrous accidents of mind.

A recurring dream that is always turning obscene. The return to cruel taunts by the other who has perceived moist meditations through the rope. Betrayals, new resentments.

There is a remarkable limitation put upon these creatures. They are unable to count past two. During certain accesses of imbecility, this talent is reduced by half. They count to themselves: "One and one and one and one . . ." or more simply, "One."

I used to like to travel. Yes, I would preen myself for flight like some strange bird. I always tended away from coasts. I was running from the horrible shorelines and their insipid incessant crash of water. When I was younger I loved the beach until, oh, one day the water washed giant holes around my feet in the sand and then started burying them, filling them in again around my ankles as I stood and stood, frozen with horror. The waves were like the low distant thudding of someone else's heart. I was sinking into the sand. That was terrifying, and I would see with girl's eyes maniac waves beating faster and faster, someone else's heart running towards death. In love with death, I wanted to go inland.

Now: no shores, no land, no heart, no . . .

Now (and there is only now), though I love to think we are careening through space—in-between galaxies—and will soon sight some strange star . . . No! That is too terrible, too much like being at sea itself. And yet, perhaps, we do twist along the rope, are swinging each other in a complicated orbit, travelling around some larger unseen planet, swimming across each other's wake . . .

Again I talk of water and pain. I wish he weren't here. I am a little more cynical, a little less touched, a little quicker. A deft touch to the rope puts him into his fits for weeks on end. I forget to forget about victimization. A weird dyslexia makes me see things upside-down and double: two ropes, two others, a regular ménage. Now think of the possibilities. But of course, something reasons against this. I would be outnumbered. That wouldn't do at all. No, no long odds for me.

The useless thinking into space, wasted energy giving off no heat, no light. The soliloquies that have no design. Debates and memories of memories like the fading response to pain of an amputated arm. The energy given off by the bodies. They are always 96° Fahrenheit, always the temperature of a scrotum, ready for reproduction, filled with genetic material, both are always ready to shoot their load along the line . . . . ready for repercussions, filled with frenetic material, both are continuously prepared to shout their goads along the line . . .

and yet . . .

I hate your interruptions, your alternate possibilities, your little eruptions which ripple along the rope against my ripples. Not even enough sense, enough breeding to wait your turn, as though time were pressing here, and our—I laugh—our friendly uh, discussion had important things hanging on it, as though it were a terrible struggle for . . . as though you were back on stage where you used to strut and flash like a peacock, missing lines, coughing into your beard, inventing—no, not even inventing—but borrowing lines from former roles, other plays, and the audience never knew. I would see your eyes triumph in the deception, but pleading, just the wet ragged edge of 'Please,' in your eyes, 'Please, Dolores,' (was that my name?) 'Please, Dolores, don't expose me here, not in front of all these people,' so I would skip a beat and respond to Strindberg when you were playing deGhelderode. That was your last resort: your little boy, your little wet ragged edge of sniffling boyhood, the little boy who stole the synagogue cats because they were warm, the little boy who didn't want his pants-down nightmares to be true, who was never sure they weren't, who was sure they were, the little boy who always wore his pants down around his ankles and went constantly tripping.

I want to love you so badly. I know now that your experience matches mine: you too have hung from ceilings with your head up your ass, put needles into those blood vessels between thumb and forefinger, have written terrible poetry and didn't know who you were. You too had only one bright defense: that you were absent from the world. For you, as for me, that absenteeism put you more firmly in the world, made you the bright center of something, made you ignore history, give up the revolution, refuse to apologize, be hopelessly loved, made you make bad connections, ride motorcycles, live in the country, eat only vegetables, want to be old, want to die, want to be a lousy grey sac of flesh hanging nowhere on a rope against another; babbling wonderful lies, quoting poetry, recalling your life like a fiction.

I want to appropriate your biography, make it mine, make it mine twice over. Be me. Let my love make you be. Let my desire put you in the world. Let me be an idea, a wonderful revelation at the right moment:

It is morning, just dawn; you were dreaming. The sun shone off a building. The curtains then blow in the breeze. The room is strange, still distant. You don't know whose it is. Maybe there is someone else sleeping next to you. You think you feel a warm back against yours. You open your eyes. Yes, the curtains are waving slowly. The second hand of the clock slowly sweeps around once, twice again. Then you think of me. There is a little ache. It is Thursday. You wonder, 'Queer fellow.' You think, 'Infatuated. Confused.'

You see a Duncan Phyffe rocker, a desk on which are poker chips, pen, fluorescent light, money jar, many scattered papers, a woolen cap, one boot. There is an oriental carpet only inches from your face. (Your arm dangles over the edge of the bed). You see a dark wooden door, a mirror in which are a Duncan Phyffe rocker, the edge of a blowing curtain and an oriental carpet, the bed posts. A seven-year-old daughter practices her tuba. The second hand sweeps around the clock face once more, gracefully. It is not I who is next to you.
   Yes.

116

You want to speak to somebody.

Yes.

You can't remember the name of the father of the tuba player.

Yes.

You have an ache.

Yes.

You want . . .

Want?

Yes.

What do I want?

Who.

Whom do I want?

You want me. You want to love me. You think to yourself, 'He is what I want.'

No.

You say, 'I . . .'

No.

'. . . want him.'

No.

'He is right for me. He is what I want.'

No.

'No . . .'

No.

'Nobody else.'

No.

No? Please, oh please want me. Please say 'I want you,' to me. Call me . . .

Yuk.

. . . your love. Say 'I am yours.'

Ugh. Ich. Tsk. Hmf. Hah. Hah. Ha! Yuk. Not. No. You?
Ahh. Ha. Ha. Ha. Chheee.

Why?

Why what?

Why not me?

Why, you are too serious.

I am not serious.

Terribly serious, delerious with serious, severely serious, insanely serious . . .

no.

Chronically serious, infected with seriousness. I don't want to be infected.

Once, while fighting in the war, we pursued our enemies across a swamp. Finally, after fourteen terrible miles, we reached a plantation. A rubber planter under special protection of the government lived there in aristocratic elegance on columned porches, amid crystal decanters, on some of the most fertile land in the world. We were struck down one by one by snipers left behind to slow us down. Occasionally, we would sight one of them and shoot to kill the bastard. Leeches crawled under your pants. In constant pain, we couldn't stop long enough to burn them off. When we finally caught up with them it was at the plantation. We saw the enemy fleeing across the lawn of the mansion, around the manicured hedges, behind the gazebo, the white wrought iron lawn furniture. The planter, all in white, leaned against the wooden column as though this sport was for his entertainment.

Two muddy and disgusted dying soldiers crossed his lawn, my buddy and I. His daughter was standing behind him, all in crinoline and lace, a dazzling white girl, about sixteen years old, her breasts almost completely exposed by her low-cut summer dress which swept down to the floor. I ran past her and dove for cover behind a hedge as shots rang out. Wriggling on my belly, I looked up to her. She winked at me and smiled. My buddy was shot in the leg and screamed out. She turned to go as her father motioned her inside. But, turning, she thought better, and pirouetting behind her father's back she faced me, lifting her skirts so she wouldn't trip, lifting her skirts higher, higher still, up to her chin until I could see the dark patch between her legs, the thighs separated and the hair glistening with moisture: the impossible promise of wet hours.

We had them surrounded. The sergeant called us back, though, because they had taken refuge among the orderly row of trees, and our government paid the planter an undisclosed sum of money for every tree wounded by our bullets.

This is the war from which I wrote you letters, letters that went unanswered. No, that should have gone unanswered as an accurate measure of your indifference. But you were too weak. You played your role. Too weak to hurt me finally, you administered small doses of pain, writing appropriate responses to hopeless letters. In short, you fanned my hopes, which rose from the stinking mud of my soul, an antediluvian beast, hungry with ages, ready to devour whole forests of love, its brainless unblinking head rearing, its enormous jaws yawning . . . I hallucinated on the primitive drugs of the jungle, projected my love against the great canvas of a jungle war. I was a silent, dutiful tin soldier for history.

You, you lived at home, spread your thighs for peace, hallucinated on the sophisticated laboratory chemicals, projected your indifference onto the blackboards of the university, seduced your professors, laughed with your friends over my letters. You wore third-hand army uniforms.

I came home. My hair was too short. I had a trigger finger. I was infectious with the taint of death. I limped from shrapnel in my ass, which endeared me to the women in bars but embarrassed you.

Whose memories are these that intrude so rashly? That set the rope to humming its awful tune? What bad novelist wrote that story? What world does he live in? How distant is it from this place where two beings float uselessly across a line from each

119

other? Does that world hang in emerald beauty somewhere not far from here? Are there answers to these questions? Is there an end to questioning? Is this space in the same space scientists write about with their equations? . . . that space the dream of generations? Does that make this a science fiction? A science? A fiction? Whose satellites are they if not of each other? Are they not unlike twin burnt-out stars, grey dwarves of collapsed form, imploded energy?

Perhaps they are enormous beings, word- and world-consuming, and they have grown out of the natural world, expanded out of the universe through some fierce mental agency. The rope between them stretches along eons of light years. They are larger than whole galaxies and don't know it. Now we are getting into the real sci-fi stuff.

The beings send stories to each other. The harmlessness of the stories. Their guise as entertainment. The way they conceal their fugitive resentments by little pointed memories created to puncture the other's armor. Their lack of memories. The immanence of their being. Their inability to be in the world. Their creation of fictions: blatant, patent lies to replace their lost memories. The failure of their desire. Their desire to fail.

Does desire fail?
    Is failure desired?
Are we allowed to be self-critical or self-conscious?
    Do you mean, 'Is that part of the author's intention?'
Yes, I think so. I think that's what I mean.
    No. The answer is no.
Someone has fucked up then.
    Not me.
Not me.
Not me.

3. Tug-of-War

He is really quite vain about the smoothness of his exoderm. I mean the way he stays out there as though he were lost in self-contemplation, absorbed in inner reflection, hypnotised by narcissism perfectly still, not budging at all, set against an eternal night (maybe that is some backdrop for a Hollywood set. Maybe this is some strange test. Maybe I am being auditioned for an upcoming role, and the strange tight-fitting costume that they've given me, closing up my mouth, my ears, my eyes, plugging and removing all the apertures but one, and in that one they stuck a terrible hair all

She seems awfully composed, as though she were waiting for me to make up my mind, make some mistake, slip up, betray my secrets. She's terriby vain. Her vanity and her watchfulness frighten me into silence. I am afraid to move, afraid motion would display my weak flank to her enmity, and all my flanks are weak, afraid motion would signal to her something unknown and terrible, and she would unleash her emotional hoard on me. Ah! The tyranny of emotion! She is bound to misconstrue me at all points— or worse—she might discover *this in order to test my endurance, my composure under duress, the range of my emotions under limited conditions, my watchfulness). I am waiting for some clue, some cue. I will know it when I see it. It will come from HIM. Yet, he remains there stonily, unyielding, with imperious silence, domineering and sadistic in his unwavering strength of will.*

If only I could be like him—to have the same skin so utterly and wonderfully grey as he has reported it to me through the rope. (Or is his a costume too?) Ah, to be self-sufficient, competent, integrated, as he appears to be . . . And I, I twist and tug and try to tumble end over end, though at best I can only rotate a few degrees from this stand stock still stasis, always trying to show him my best face. He rarely responds, and when he does, it is briefly, explosively . . . to take me in a torrent of words, tugs, violent jabs from the rope, terrible twistings which violate me in the worst way, which make the hair up my anus twitter and rub for unbearable seconds, an irritation which must seek relief . . . and just when I think I must explode . . . it is over, passing away like a dream of a shadow, and he is on the end, again, back out there on our limp life-line impassive as ever, and the

the hidden intents, the fugitive resentments, the subconscious hostilities, the utter revulsion I feel at the sight of her, the proximity of her, the hate of the irrevocable thread which has bound our fates together.

Somehow I have forgotten though if we are here by choice or not. Somehow, I feel that would make a difference—not as though I could then unchoose—no, I am not so optimistic. But then it would appear that this is a burden which I feel would yield some rewards. We are so different. Yet, I would like to be like her: independent, forceful, outspoken.

Yes, I find my rewards. In the end it is wonderfully rewarding to stay here, wherever we are, almost anonymous and just silently be. Just be. To go down deep beyond boredom itself (that boredom around which all life orbits). And when I am forced to respond to her, and I respond reluctantly, I am certain, it is wildly, out of fear. My mind is like a cornered dog and snaps out in brief but violent ways. I try to hurt her by plunging the intentions of a maniac into the very seat of her pulpy mass. At this time a part of me always coolly reasons, and I watch myself per-

hair in my hole is talking now, whispering like a little rope, a miniature but intimate imitation, speaking its insistent dissatisfactions to me. How can I help but be sensitive, hurt? How can I help but feel put-upon, abused, frustrated and discarded? As though I hardly existed, or I existed as some ancillary organ, an auxiliary attachment to his rope. It wasn't like this when I was a little girl. I wasn't bred and brought up to become a monstrous freak. THIS IS NOT THE WAY IT WAS SUPPOSED TO BE!

Look, this hurts me too. We only have each other. But even this he finds hard to absorb. He twists it all around, uses my words against me: "What do you mean, screwed up?" Then he goes all crazy.

I annoy him. I know it. I am terribly annoying. I shout at him for little things, and he becomes less responsive. I become even more irritating, and he becomes like a ghost, only a not-thereness. I go all ugly. He disappears. Then I am lost. Then I fear the flight into an ocean of need, like the beach slipping away from around my feet, washed out to sea. Reference points are gone . . .

form so indecently upon her; I always wonder why she seems most vulnerable, most yielding, even while she screams, though I cannot hear. Maybe that is merely my masculine fantasy. I try to hurt her, and the rope jabs my manic message into her: NO DAMMIT IF YOU WANT ATTENTION, THIS IS WHAT YOU GET YOU WHOREDAUGHTER MOONCALF YOU PIGPUCKERED GIBBON'S TEAT, YOU REAMER YOU REIVER YOU BEAVER YOU FLAMING FAT-FACED FROWSY FLIT, YOU SLITSICK CHANCRE, YOU VENEREAL-LICKED LESION LIPPER, YOU DOG-DUNG DIPPER . . . And then I am done. Before she can reply or try to reciprocate—I am back behind my shield of silence, my catatonic cloak. It's not exactly what I would call fair, but it is very exciting. Those are exciting moments. The hair in my ass dances, burrowing even deeper, then springing out, slithering around in the empty space like, why, very like a rope. Still, my fear grows back on me, redoubled by the pain of my recent pleasures, the twinges of remorse attendant upon them. DOES IT HAVE TO BE LIKE THIS? Must I make sporadic forays into her because I am afraid, confined, disgus-

But this was all a delusion. I know now what time is like, and that all my dreams of finally sprouting moving things to propel me, inner wirings to replace the rope, organs of perception and expression . . . all of which I have seen so vividly, all the dreams of which I took for prophesy and premonition, something promised me by the universe—all these were wispy deceptions, hallucinations, or worse, memories of lives that could not be again. Now it is too late, he sees what I am like and he cannot, does not, want me, want me to want him, want me to want him to want me to want him to . . .

Once—no, maybe several times— he wanted me to want him. I said no, I couldn't. I was holding out for something far better, deep down I thought he was O.K., but we were too much alike, and in the end, at bottom, I figured . . . no this can't go on. This is a bad dream. Life isn't always going to be like this. This is a strange, savage phase which I'll grow out of, and then what use would he be to me? Could you imagine me intro-

ted, closed? Why in this infinite beautiful blackness must I feel so claustrophobic, restrained by her madness? Two points and a line may determine an entire universe. Here they only determine the overwhelming desire to merge with darkness, to become a greater more silent nothing.

Sometimes I venture tendernesses. Are you awright? I ask. What's wrong? I ask. Why are you so screwed up? Why is the rope so tight? C'mon, leave a little slack. Oh, please, it will make things so much easier on both of us. Look, this hurts me, too. We only have each other. But even this she finds hard to absorb, like . . . well, she twists it all around, uses my words against me: "What do you mean, screwed up?" Then she goes all crazy and gives me a good rope-lashing: Tight? I'll show you what tight is like. I begin to wither up, my flesh necroses. I want to shed the skin which is distended so painfully then. All this occurs because the formalities can't work here. The rope betrays my secrets, the rope made somehow crazily sensitive by her craziness, her frailty, her vulnerability. The rope somehow protects her—from my lies, my insincerity, the false *ducing him to friends—rolling him out on an elaborate silver cart—a grey ugly lump of flesh, an unmatched scrotum? And I would have to serve him, defer to him . . . he would be demanding, irritable from the consciousness of his obvious immobility, uselessness, inferiority.*

I am unmoored, adrift, alone, but he lies. He lies so poorly, so absolutely, so unashamedly. Oh, he lies, and yet, perverse me, I blame him for not lying with greater finesse, for being such a clumsy dissimulator, for telling me what I think he wants to hear . . . what I indeed do want to hear . . . but he uses violent words, his vibrations are too strong, too aggressive. The rope hops and jerks; everything seems ambiguous. I wait for that warm sensation that signals to me that he is honest. (It takes more energy for him to tell the truth.) The gentle rippling of the rope . . . no, no . . . but instead it frays, no, no, it tries to slip away from my body, elude my grasp . . . no no . . . almost as if it had a will of its own and couldn't abide being the medium for our sordid transmissions. I could go crazy. I try to reach those moments of rare consciousness when I can pretend that

niceties I should have abandoned long ago. It hums to her in some secret way, whispering I don't know what. That's uncanny. Yes, the rope seems so much like a silent arbitrator, a silent mediator, a faithless interpreter. Untrustworthy rope! Sends the sense behind the words, resonates with an energy not my own, certainly not hers. It incarnates through some transcendent mistake my private emotional discourse; it magnifies accidents in my narration, slips that reveal my secret aggressive intentions. My hostilities. That's marvelous. Why, when we should be so sympathetic, when by the very accident of our being, our being here, our being here together we should understand each other, comply, bend and compromise so readily, why do we fail? It feels like some other agent is writing this story, is scripting this scenario that always tends so ineluctably towards failure. Someone maliciously, terribly cruel is interceding, disrupting the normal train of events, twisting our lives in incomprehensible knots. For who, who can believe in the end, at bottom, that they are finally responsible for their own botched lives? Maybe the rope is our taunting manipulating god.

I am alone and that the suffering Yet how can that be? I am
here is only a reflection of my losing it. It is so much langu-
beauty, don't lose it now . . . I age itself, like pure self like,
must try to gain control . . . think . . . imply . . . what? Perhaps we
are products of ITS imagination. We recite mantras to regain our
calm, to forget about the rope . . . **To love the love that loves**
to love the love that loves to love. To love the loves that
love to love the loves that love to love. To love the love
that loves to love the love that loves to love . . . No buts
no jokes no doubts about it . . . we reach to those rare
moments of consciousness, ingenuousness. True but three is a
crowd . . . Ladies! Hold the door open for your men! One
moment . . . which one of us is talking here? One can forget
who is speaking is speaking. I mean, just let . . . no, *I* mean,
just let me . . . yes, let the rope take over. When the words
must just come. We are mediums for self-consciousness; mere
vibrators: twenty-five cents a hot hit. Just lie down, two-bits,
shake-em-up; we're oscillating idiots, peculiarly adaptable,
highly specialized machines designed for one purpose only: to
speak our minds. That's what makes us truly grotesque,
monstrous. AM I THE SPEAKER OR THE SPOKEN? WHO IS
TALKING RIGHT NOW? WHO IS TALKING, GODDAM-
MIT? I WANT TO KNOW. To know to know to know. **The**
doppelganger mirror to deep unutterable plottings . . .
the infinitely needy most desirous mask of a mask . . .
the inner dismay at his yearnings . . . **See how I've been**
corrupted . . . **preparing me for the beginning of a new**
cycle . . . **leaked human effort back into the natural**
universe . . . **it was the oldest story in the world** . . . **a**
gross insensitive affair . . . **Yet, no light, no heat nor the**
perceptible lack thereof . . . **animal pressures on the**
brain . . . **pucker squirm close clamp glisten rub osculate**
pout vibrate emit suck . . . **sequestered and strange**
beings . . . **a fluttering but continuous importance** . . .
the fear that . . . **a rift in understanding for which the**
victim is responsible . . . **a small ripe crease** . . . **sordid**
and incomplete transmissions. Please.

The strange doubts concerning identity. The phases of utter self-consciousness which consume intelligence and reduce it to babbling insanity. The fear that the rope only truly exists, and that they are mere figments, fictions, stories told to itself.

FICTION COLLECTIVE
Books in Print:

The Second Story Man by Mimi Albert
Althea by J. M. Alonso
Searching for Survivors by Russell Banks
Babble by Jonathan Baumbach
Reruns by Jonathan Baumbach
Things in Place by Jerry Bumpus
Ø Null Set by George Chambers
Amateur People by Andrée Connors
Take It or Leave It by Raymond Federman
Museum by B. H. Friedman
Temporary Sanity by Thomas Glynn
The Talking Room by Marianne Hauser
Holy Smoke by Fanny Howe
Mole's Pity by Harold Jaffe
Moving Parts by Steve Katz
Find Him! by Elaine Kraf
Reflex and Bone Structure by Clarence Major
The Secret Table by Mark Mirsky
Encores for a Dilettante by Ursule Molinaro
Rope Dances by David Porush
The Broad Back of the Angel by Leon Rooke
The Comatose Kids by Seymour Simckes
Fat People by Carol Sturm Smith
The Hermetic Whore by Peter Spielberg
Twiddledum Twaddledum by Peter Spielberg
98.6 by Ronald Sukenick
Meningitis by Yuriy Tarnawsky
Statements 1
Statements 2

Fiction Collective books, catalogues, and subscription information may be obtained directly by mail from: Coda Press, Inc., 700 West Badger Road, Suite 101, Madison, WI 53713. Bookstores: Order through George Braziller, Inc., One Park Avenue, New York, NY 10016.